A SAVAGE ACT

PATTI GRIFFIN

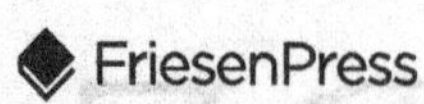

One Printers Way
Altona, MB R0G 0B0
Canada

www.friesenpress.com

First Edition — 2021

Author photograph: Chelsea Boyd Gibson

ISBN
978-1-03-912199-7 (Hardcover)
978-1-03-912198-0 (Paperback)
978-1-03-912200-0 (eBook)

1. FICTION, LITERARY

Distributed to the trade by The Ingram Book Company

For my brother Peter.

In my eyes you are a warrior. Your fight opened my heart to life's most precious gifts. Thank you for your brave journey.

When the ordinary is disrupted, the exception can occur.

Prologue

The British Columbia temperate rainforest is one of the last true wilderness areas remaining on Earth. This vast, lush ecosystem has been standing, breathing, and generously providing for hundreds of years. A prolific number of species thrive on its rich nourishment and safe cover. It witnesses and it hides without condition or judgement.

Today it is a way out.

“Be quiet. Run as fast as you can and don’t stop for anything.”

Robbie is shocked by what they are about to do but has little time to ponder when he’s plucked from his thoughts by the strong grip of his brother’s hand. The ten-year-old follows RJ into the forest like an obedient pup, intense fear choking back his tears. It is a huge gamble. No one has successfully escaped. Those who have tried wished they hadn’t.

RJ stops near a large cedar and unearths two small backpacks. He takes a flashlight out of one and secures the pack on Robbie’s back. He quickly puts the other on his own back, pulling it tight. So far, they’ve gone undetected. Dinner, as meagre as it is, hasn’t been served yet, and if they are lucky, their absence may go unnoticed for a while longer.

RJ firmly takes his brother by the shoulders. Robbie seems much smaller than he ought to be. “Robbie, I know you’re scared.

I'm scared, too, but we have to do this. If we don't get out of here, we're going to end up like Edward."

Robbie nods.

Edward was his best friend. He wasn't able to learn the prayers or stop crying when he was told to—he missed his family too much. He was strapped by the supervisor and spent mealtimes in the attic. He eventually became sick.

Now, Edward is buried in the field behind the big Douglas fir. Robbie sometimes visits his grave during lunch. He made sure he could always tell it from the others by sticking a soup spoon in the ground at the foot of the mound. He chose the strongest and shiniest spoon he could find and hammered it with a rock until only the bowl stuck out. Even when the weeds set in, he would count fifty steps from the tree, and there was his spoon at Edward's feet.

Robbie found it odd that no one went to see Edward, not even when he was sick. He died alone in the infirmary.

"You must keep up with me. And no stopping until I say."

Robbie feels like he is in a dream, except he can feel his heart pounding and his throat getting tight. This isn't a dream. It's real. They are going to run.

"Are you listening to me, Robbie? This is our only chance."

Fear grips his voice. "Yes."

"OK, let's go."

The autumn light will soon fade, and the miniature torch won't help much in the dark, dense bush, but it's something. They have to make it past the old hunters' camp, go off trail into the bush, and make a steep climb into the old growth.

The two boys keep a frantic pace, running and dodging stumps, rocks, and thick undergrowth for hours. They know they will need a significant head start to outrun the dogs and rage that will unfold behind them.

Robbie trips and falls into a tree, scratching his cheek and covering his palms and fingers in sticky sap. The forest smells good.

He knows this could end badly but decides it's worth the risk. He wonders where they are heading and if anyone will help them. He's sure his brother has a plan. They cannot end up like Edward.

He wipes his hands on his pants, straightens up, and starts running again, quickly catching sight of his brother. This time, he has no problem keeping up despite his new welts and bruises. They can't hurt him now, not tonight. Tonight, he is like the great bear—powerful, fast, and undeterred.

Don't stop, don't look back, just keep going.

They are free.

Three Years Later

Twenty-six-year-old Julie Morneau pulls into the parking lot overlooking Nora Beach and speaks into her radio. "What time was it called in?"

"Ah, that would be twenty-one twenty-two," replies Sadie.

"Response time?" Julie asks. No answer. "When was the response time, Sadie?"

"Um, hold on. Sergeant Wylie responded at twenty-one fifty. I haven't heard from him, so he must still be there."

"Roger that. Thanks, Sadie. Damn, Wylie. That's just what I need."

The constable steps out of patrol car six and scans the familiar surroundings she has grown to love since she was a child. She tucks her curly red locks behind her ears and straightens her uniform. The sound of the surf saturates the air; the amber on the horizon has all but slipped away. She takes the familiar stairs to the sand and heads north. Smoke and a few lingering bystanders hover in the distance. Julie feels her heart thumping as she begins to recognize the area.

Her heavy boots sink into the fine sand with each step, slowing her from reaching the unfolding scene. An ambulance silently bounces along the beach, heading north, its lights flashing. Just ahead, a fire smolders, blurring the remnants of a small teepee.

Two black SUVs are positioned with their headlights facing the scene.

Julie's mind races, trying to make sense of what she is seeing. She catches the attention of a couple who are mournfully walking away. They make eye contact, as if wanting to speak, but Julie doesn't slow down. She clumsily sprints up to Sergeant Wylie, who is surveying the scene and scratching notes into a small notepad.

"What happened here?" she asks. "Where's the owner?"

The wind has picked up, making the strong surf even louder. Wylie stops what he is doing and looks at the rookie disrupting his scene. "There's an owner? What do you know about it?"

"Well, nothing, really. I believe a man lived here. What happened?"

Wylie stops writing and leans closer to hear Julie over the crashing waves. "Did you know him?"

"Yes. I mean, no, I don't know him, exactly. His name is Daiji. He's a quiet Indigenous man in his forties, maybe?"

"Who is he? What was he doing here?" asks Wylie.

"I didn't get his full story. Some of the surfers said he was on a traditional journey of some kind but enjoyed this beach, so they built him the teepee."

"Well, that's just great. Why don't we build little huts for every bum that makes his way to the beach," Wylie says mockingly. "There's not much left to it now."

They both look at the burning logs.

"If he's transient, he's an easy target out here," Wylie says. "Someone obviously knew that and thought it might be fun to torch his illegal stick house and knock him around. The guy is pretty beat up and was left for dead."

Julie covers her mouth, lets out a heavy sigh, and walks toward the smoldering pile of debris. She has only been with the force for three years and prides herself on being as tough as any seasoned officer, but unprovoked cruelty is hard to process.

Wylie follows her and makes an attempt at sensitivity. "Tell me what you know about him."

Julie regains her composure and looks directly at her superior officer. "Is he alive?"

"Barely. A couple out for a walk found him about an hour ago." Wylie points to the taped off area in the sand. "He was lying here, outside of this structure, unconscious and bleeding."

"You think he pulled himself out?"

"Or someone else did," says Wylie. "See these marks here? It looks like he was dragged."

Julie focuses on the marks in the sand. They are covered in blood.

"Someone dragged him out but left him bleeding? That doesn't make sense."

"It rarely does," Wylie says, scanning the beach. "Probably kids hopped up on meth, crack, or God knows what."

"Or someone pulled him out but didn't want to be involved," says Julie.

"He may have been hit when the structure collapsed but it looked like there was foul play. He had marks on his face and torso indicating an assault. They called the ambulance and fire department. He's on his way to Ramsey General."

"Any leads?" she asks.

"Yeah, you! I've been here less than an hour." Wylie looks around at the few dispersing bystanders. "No one here knows anything, not even a name, except you and one of the surfers."

"I knew him by Daiji because that's all he told me."

"You spoke to him?"

"Yes, I spoke to him once. He was a loner. He wasn't a drinker or a delinquent. He said he used to go canoeing and liked the beach. Some of the surfers said he was a shaman."

Sergeant Wylie slowly blows out a breath, likely to prevent an eruption. He has clearly reached his sensitivity quota for the day.

"He's a decent guy," Julie continues, looking at the ash pile. "He certainly didn't deserve this."

Sergeant Wylie steps back with eyes squinting and lips pursed, like a dog defending its bone. "Go back to the station, Morneau, and think about what you have for me. I have to talk to forensics here and then I will be back to talk to you."

Julie heads for the stairs. She glances back to catch a glare of contempt before continuing down the beach.

Ramsey Police Department

Ramsey PD is located on the rocky west edge of town, with a bird's eye view of the harbor. The low-key tourist town barely registers two thousand residents most months but grows many times that size during the summer surf season.

Most Ramsey crimes are petty but occasionally an anomaly occurs, like the ambitious young sailor who smuggles illegal substances into the harbor or the one-off biker deal that goes gorily wrong. Ramsey's low criminal gloss and location on the Pacific west tip can, on occasion, leave it ripe for a potential crime mystery.

Julie sits silently at her desk, poring over the scene in her mind. *How could such a senseless, violent crime not draw attention? Someone, somewhere, must know something!*

She decides to go back to Nora Beach and talk to the surfers. They press their luck until dusk and linger for hours, so someone may have seen something unusual. Her thoughts are interrupted by the arrival of the Wyle Man, as he is known by junior officers who are all too familiar with his affinity for humiliation.

"OK, Morneau, in my office," he shouts as he blows past her. Julie quickly follows him to his office and takes a seat. "Tell me what I need to know and don't leave anything out."

"Well, sir, I knew the man in question through his reputation with the surfers."

"Surfers?"

"Yes, sir, I do a little surfing myself, and he's known on the beach as a kind, quiet man. The surfers say he used to do some paddling in his younger years. He's a kind soul and was on a spiritual journey of sorts. I don't remember the nation he's from but I'm pretty sure he's a respected elder." Julie pauses and debates whether the conversation will make it through Wylie's jaded, thick skull. "He's a shaman, a healer, spiritual guy."

"Yes, you mentioned that. Did you ask him if he had a permit for his shack, by any chance?"

"No, sir, I didn't ask for a permit. I did suggest that he consider checking in with the shelter."

"Great, Morneau, you gave him a suggestion. That was very nice of you. What if he's a criminal or there's a warrant out on him? Why is he living on a beach? You know, Morneau, the mayor is cracking down on these tent cities and the like. These people have to get jobs and pay rent like everyone else."

"Yes, sir, I am aware of the mayor's perspective."

"But you chose to look the other way, Morneau, is that right? You do remember you're a police constable, do you not?"

"Yes, sir, I do. I just thought he was trying to do something helpful here. He wanted to share his traditions with the kids along the coast. It didn't sound like he would be here long. There was a bigger picture here, sir."

"Oh, a bigger picture? I see, Morneau," Wylie says mockingly. "Then maybe he should have stayed at the Sheridan. That'll be all, Morneau. You can share the big picture with Brooks and Hannah. They will be working the case."

"But sir, I know the area and the people. I was second on the scene. I should do this!"

"No, Morneau, you shouldn't. If you had done your job correctly the first time, there wouldn't be any need for an investigation."

Sergeant Wylie gets up from his desk, walks toward Julie, and leans so close she can smell his sour coffee breath.

"Believe me, I'm doing you a favor. You're getting off easy." He straightens his tie and walks out, leaving Julie alone in his office.

She slumps in the chair where many others have slumped before and bites her lip, breathing through the burning in her stomach.

Nora Beach

Nora Beach is known for endless white sand, a big surf, and plenty of amped riders looking for a rip.

Julie lies on her stomach, paddling and bobbing in the waves. She ducks the shorebreak and positions herself in the lineup. This is exactly what she needs to release the toxic build-up of Wylie tampering with her brain.

She gazes at the endless line of A-frames heading her way. She hops on her board, shifts too much to the right, and is forced to bail. The strong offshore wind is whipping up a bad chop, leaving balance and timing to the gods. The surf is pulled and pounded by the strong gusts, leaving Julie in a spin cycle of dive and tumble. She shakes it off and paddles her way to shore.

"You're taking some dirty lickings there, Julie."

"Hey, Podster, I know it. My head isn't in it. I came to blow off steam but I'm grubbing on everyone."

"Well, the crosswind isn't helping any. Maybe it's a thrashing you're looking for." Podster laughs.

She smirks. "I'm certainly getting it, then."

"Hard day, was it?" asks Podster.

Julie nods.

"Did you hear about the shaman?"

"Yes, I did. I was at the scene but so far, we have no leads. Did anyone see anything?"

Podster looks out at the surf and shakes his head. "No one has been here for days. It's been nothing but mush. I have been asking around, but no one knows anything. Is he going to make it, Julie?"

"He's fighting. According to Ramsey Health Centre, he has a serious head injury. He was stable but unresponsive, so they transferred him to Chelsey for further assessment."

"Ah, yes, he's fighting," says Podster. "Crossing between two worlds, healing himself this time."

Julie smiles at the surfer's sincerity. Podster spent a lot of time with Daiji. The shaman has become a respected elder among the surfers.

"I'll keep my ears open," says Podster. "If anyone knows anything, I'll let you know."

"Thank you. I appreciate that."

Julie gathers her board and walks to her Jeep to grab her change of clothes. She pulls off her water shoes and pushes her feet into her runners. She peels off her suit and replaces it with a pair of shorts and a T-shirt. Before leaving, she decides to take a walk to the scene.

Clean-up was thorough, leaving very little of the healing hut, as the surfers affectionately referred to it. Julie sits on a nearby log, contemplating the scene. Who would do this? It doesn't make sense. Daiji didn't have anything anyone would want. He didn't accept cash and lived on offerings of kindness, which he returned tenfold with his compassionate listening and storytelling. Why would anyone want to hurt him?

Julie collects her thoughts, stands, and begins to return to her Jeep when she notices a teenage boy at the lookout, gazing down at the charred remains of Daiji's home.

"Hello!" Julie shouts to him. "Did you know the man who lived here?"

The boy looks up, startled, and quickly walks away in the other direction. Julie shouts again: "Hey, wait a minute. I just want to talk!" She heads toward the stairs and sprints to the top, but the kid is gone.

Ramsey Police Department

Sergeants Anthony Brooks and Michael Hannah have full command of Ramsey PD's briefing room. Officers from all shifts have been asked for any leads on the recent assault at Nora Beach. Brooks reads from a report received from Ramsey General.

"Blunt force trauma to the head, multiple contusions on the face, head, and torso, as well as several broken ribs. Injuries are indicative of an assault. The report says he is stable and has moderate brain activity but is not responding to verbal commands. A CT scan does not show anything conclusive. Glasgow coma scale is eleven, which translates to moderate severity, whatever that means. He has been transferred to Chelsey.

"It is a wait and see status for this man, but either way, he probably won't be the same again. Whoever he is, as no one seems to know anything about him. He had no identification on him, no last address, nothing. He is basically homeless."

Julie takes notes at the back of the room. She understands what a file tagged "homeless" means. Practically speaking, no one really cares and not much effort goes into finding someone who does. At least Brooks is in charge—he's decent.

Julie raises her head. "He was known," she says.

"What was that?" asks Brooks.

"Constable Morneau, Sergeant. I met Daiji once, but some of the surfers know him well. He's a storyteller and shaman. They built him a shelter on the beach. He seemed like a good man, a Native healer. No one really bothered him until now."

"You knew Daiji? You had contact?"

"One time, yes."

"Good. Where's he from?"

"I don't know, exactly. He wasn't local but he did say he was from the coast, so I'm thinking one of the Salish or Nuu-chah-nulth nations?"

"Did he mention family? Last name, perhaps?"

"No, he didn't. I plan to talk with some of the locals at the beach to find out more."

"Good. Thank you, Constable Morneau." Brooks walks toward Julie and studies her young face. "Please get back to me on that."

"Yes, sir," she says, keeping eye contact.

"Next time, asking a few more questions would be prudent. Check with some of the reserves to see if they know anything. For tomorrow morning?"

"I will try my best, sir."

"Good. That's what I need to hear. We need everyone's best. This case could blow up very fast. The word is out about this incident and people are getting worked up. It's violence. Violence against a homeless person, maybe First Nations.

"There's a group from the coast—the Tla-o-qui-aht Nation—gathering as we speak. Maybe he's from their area. There are activists on the west side wanting to use this as a platform to highlight homelessness in the area. That is likely to provoke some lively debate.

"Our public relations team is trying to contain this, but we have to find out more about who this guy is, where his family is, and who did this. Constable Thomas will be giving a statement later today. We are calling it a random act against a vulnerable man. He didn't have proper housing. We can't protect people if we don't know they exist."

"The Housing Association will love that," one of the officers moans.

Brooks pauses, looks at the cynic in the crowd, and continues. "Like I said, we have to do our due diligence here. People are scared. When people get scared, they talk, so keep your ears open and ask questions everywhere. I know we are busy here. If this is not your case, then keep it in the back of your mind. We want you to give a shit!"

He has their attention. Anthony Brooks can inspire. A proud second-generation Black Canadian man, raised by a hard-working immigrant family. The course of his life was changed forever when his younger brother was murdered by a gang member in Vancouver. He turned down a life in law to work directly with communities, volunteering his precious time off with local youth groups.

His recent move to the coast is an attempt to transition to the idea of retirement, which so far has not been successful. He is well respected in the department. A compliment from Brooks can be career-changing, and it's sought after by every ambitious rookie eager to please, except for Julie.

Julie doesn't quite fit the pleasing mold. She instead pursues the odd dream of protecting the innocent. While not opposed to climbing the ranks, she intends to prove her worth on the way there.

"We are putting an extra police presence around the beach. Sergeant Hannah will coordinate that with a couple of officers later," Brooks says. "OK, that's it for now. Be back here tomorrow morning."

Press Briefing

The pressroom at Ramsey Police Department does not see much action. The local daily has its usual spot, but today, a few curious reporters with microphones and disposable coffee cups have joined in. A TV crew from the city has made the trip, along with coastal radio and a couple of small-town news outlets all hoping for a beachside mystery.

Constable Reginald Thomas is surprised by the extra bodies. He takes his position behind the podium, spies the camera, and straightens his tie.

"Ahem. Good afternoon. My name is Constable Reginald Thomas, and I am here to report what we know about the recent assault on Nora Beach. The incident took place sometime between nineteen hours and twenty-one hours on Saturday, July 27.

"Our victim is a male of Indigenous origin, approximately forty to fifty years of age. He goes by the name Daiji and has no known last name. He suffered a blunt force head injury, likely caused by an assault and the collapse of a teepee-like structure he was living in. He is stable but still in a coma. If anyone has any information regarding this individual, his family, or where he is from, please contact the Ramsey Police Department."

One of the reporters in the scrum speaks up.

"Josie Perkins from Coastal News," she says. "Constable, isn't there a town bylaw prohibiting structures on the beach?"

"Yes, there is. The city and the police were not aware of the structure."

"How long was the teepee there?"

"I can't answer that exactly. It may have been there for a couple of weeks. We are not sure. It was on the north end, where there is less traffic. It went unnoticed until now."

"Constable, are there any suspects?" says another reporter. "Mark Brown from the Pilot."

"No, not yet."

Robert Groomer from the local paper sits in the front row. He raises his hand to catch the constable's attention.

"Robert Groomer from the Chronicle. Constable Thomas do you think this is a result of the housing crisis extending from the city to the coastal areas and the fact that we're throwing our seniors in the street?"

"Robert Groomer, how nice of you to join us," Thomas says. "I would say that is a stretch, Robert. We know very little about the assault at this point or why it occurred."

"Could it be related to any of the gangs that pass through at this time of year?" asks Groomer.

"Like I said, it's early in the investigation, but there's no reason to suspect that."

"BSR Radio. Constable, do we know what nation this man is from?"

"We think he's from the Nuu-chah-nulth people, but we don't know where exactly. We are hoping the public will be able to help us with that."

"Josie Perkins again, Constable Thomas. There is a rumor that some of the kids from the youth home may have been involved. Is that the direction you're going?"

"That is a rumor—in fact, one I haven't heard. Stick to the facts, please. This is a crime, an assault, and maybe a random act of violence." Thomas gathers his papers and tucks them under his arm. "That's it for now. Thank you."

Julie

From the cliffs above the beach, Julie looks out at the sixteen kilometres of white sand hugging the edge of the Pacific. The surfers and sand worshippers are soaking up the final cherished days of the summer. It's hard to believe it could be the scene of a violent crime. The thought barely leaves her mind when she notices someone breaking away from the crowd and walking toward the staircase below her.

Ugh, Robert Groomer. What is he up to now? She ignores his wave and turns toward the Boardwalk café. *This may be a good time for lunch.*

The café is a bustling favourite with tourists and locals alike. The owner Doris Hopkins is busy taking orders behind the counter.

"Hey, Doris, how are you today?"

"Good day, Constable Morneau. I'm just fine. How are things?"

"Pretty good." Julie takes a stool at the counter. "Can I please get my regular veggie on rye and a double shot Americano please?"

"You sure can." Doris writes down the order and sends it to the kitchen. "Any news about the assault on the beach?"

"No, Doris. Nothing yet, I'm afraid."

"I hear people talking. They say it's not safe out there."

"People exaggerate, but we have put an extra car on the boardwalk."

Julie sips her coffee and reviews her notes.

"You're being followed." Doris nods at the reporter entering the café and making his way toward Julie.

Julie smiles, still ignoring the intruder. "I know," she says. Without turning around, she speaks to him. "I have nothing for you, Robert. That's what the press briefing was for."

"What brings you here, Constable Morneau?" he says. "I thought you might have gathered more information, since you've been questioning people all morning."

Julie looks directly at Robert, who has secured a spot close to her. Annoyingly close. "I wasn't questioning. I was chatting. There's a difference. And how would you know what I've been doing?"

"It's what any responsible officer would do, don't you think?"

Robert continues to push his luck. "Do you think it's one of the kids from Shannon House?"

Julie struggles to remain patient with the pushy reporter. "Like you were told today, we don't know what this is. We are talking to people and looking for witnesses. That's protocol. Why would you think someone from Shannon House was involved?"

"Well, some of our concerned citizens have theories. Speaking of which, you should probably know that some of those fine folks are meeting at the community centre tonight to discuss these theories in depth."

Julie sighs. "We are aware. We want to get to the bottom of this as much as they do," she says.

Robert nods, stands, and heads for the door.

"Robert!" Julie shouts. "Let me know if there are any sparks at this gathering of concerned folks. You know what I mean."

Robert laughs. "You can read about it, officer. That's what the news is for."

"Oh, is that what it's for?" she says. "Could have fooled me."

Julie finishes her sandwich outside, pacing the boardwalk and contemplating the theories that will likely come up among the overanxious imaginations at the town meeting. She returns to her car to hear her radio buzzing her name.

"Morneau, are you there?"

"Morneau here."

"Morneau, this is Sergeant Brooks."

"Hello, sir. What can I do for you?"

"I would like you to follow up on a tip we received from the youth home on the east side."

"You mean Shannon House?"

"Yes, that's the one. You need to talk to Eugene. He's one of the youth workers. He reports a couple of the kids were acting strangely on the night in question. Let me know what you get."

"Yes, sir."

Daiji

A low pressure has moved in, bringing a warm stillness to the inlet. A cloud-capped sky hovers over the grey-blue glass of Rubin Bay as determined sunbeams pirouette across its surface. It is a work of art.

Daiji takes a break from paddling and leans back in the hollow of his craft, one hand dipping into the cool water at his side. He has been away too long. He breathes in the sweet smells of cotton-wood and fir that drift up from the rocky shore. He tastes the salty air. The stunning array of life and colour drench his consciousness. Yellow cushions of algae pop against the grey-blue canvas of rock and water, nestled among fluorescent green lichen and meandering purple starfish.

This is where I need to be.

He is the only one around for miles, but far from alone. His smooth, steady strokes are followed by his many companions, who swoop and bob alongside him. They have no demands; they are masters of a life humans endeavour to find.

Today he breathes with them again. Just breathe.

Shannon House

Shannon House is a rectangular building that sits on twenty acres of property just north of Nora Beach. The austere concrete structure was built in the fifties and was used for the detention and custody of "misguided" youth aged sixteen years and under who were found guilty of delinquency.

These wayward souls were forced back on track by the motherland, which saw to their educational, industrial, and moral training. Fifteen years after it opened, the industrial school was accused of losing sight of "the child's best interest." The facility was promptly closed and taken over by Child and Family Services.

A middle aged woman is sifting through papers at a desk in the front office. She stops what she's doing and stands to greet Julie.

"Hello officer. I'm Mabel Harper. We were expecting you."

"Hello, I'm Constable Morneau. Thank you for seeing me, Ms. Harper."

"Of course, Constable Morneau. I understand you need to speak with Eugene."

"Yes, thank you."

Julie is led down a narrow hallway and shown into a large room with an oval table and leather chairs. There's a TV tuned to the local news, a water cooler, and a coffee station. Julie helps herself to a water and takes a seat.

Shannon House holds no resemblance to or feeling of a home, despite recent efforts to update and disguise its contentious beginnings. The residents' rooms have been improved, but the hallways and office areas retain the juvie feel. Or perhaps the trauma of the past lingers here.

A bearded man in his mid-thirties with a plaid shirt and skinny jeans appears.

"Officer Morneau. I'm Eugene. nice to meet you."

"Hello, Eugene. I was told you left a message at the station."

"Yes, I did, and I'm sorry it took me so long. I know you've been asking the public for information, but I just wasn't sure it was related. I mean, I still don't know, really."

"I understand, Eugene. We appreciate any tips. It's our job to decide whether they should be investigated further, so thank you for calling. You said you didn't know if it was related?"

"The night of the assault on Nora Beach, I was working the night shift. I heard the news a couple of days later and was reflecting on that night. We can see the beach from here. It's a distance, but some of the kids have been known to wander that way on weekends. I do remember a couple of our boys were late that night and I was worried about them because they took one of the younger girls with them—Lisa, their sister. I was about to call my supervisor when they returned."

"What time was that?"

"It must have been just after eight p.m. Lisa is supposed to be in by eight o'clock."

"So was there anything out of the ordinary?" asks Julie.

"No, not really. But I mean, I don't know. It's not the first time Jimmy and Jonathan were out late. They apologized and went to their room. That in and of itself was unusual."

"What do you mean?"

"Well, they usually tear up the kitchen for snacks or watch TV before bed, but not that night. They went straight to their rooms—well, except Jimmy. The other two went to bed. They seemed to be spooked in some way."

"What do you mean spooked?"

"Like they were up to something, or running from something. I asked if everything was OK and Jimmy said yes, he was just tired.

I assumed they were up to no good, but to be honest, I had no energy to probe further. They were in, so I let them go. I checked on Lisa, and she was changed and in bed for the night. The next day, I heard about the assault on the beach. It crossed my mind that they were involved, but then all hell broke loose, and I forgot about it until yesterday."

"What do you mean, all hell broke loose?"

"Well, one of the boys, Jimmy, ran away the next day. We checked around town, called tribal police and the RCMP, reached out to all his former foster parents and filled out endless reports, but there's no sign of him. This kid has a history, and if he doesn't want to be found, he's pretty effective at falling off the grid. We filed a missing persons report. It's been a crazy couple of days. The officer we spoke to told us to contact Sergeant Brooks about the possibility of this being related to the incident on Nora Beach, so here we are."

"You said Jimmy has a history? What did you mean by that?"

"He has gone AWOL before, and if he doesn't want to be found, he won't be. In the past, he's gone north. He is very resourceful and has spent time in the bush. The boys even changed their names at one point. Jimmy only comes back when he feels like it. If he feels like it."

"Why did they change their names?"

"Well, before they came into foster care, their lives were traumatic. They had been on the run from Indian agents, and while their birth certificates have their maternal last name, they insisted we call them by their middle names and father's last name."

"Hmm. That's unusual, isn't it?"

"When you think about it, not really. They didn't want to be found and spent time with their paternal uncle in the bush. To them, it made sense to take their father's last name. They were having difficulty adjusting, especially Jimmy, so we went along with it. We do whatever we can to reduce a kid's trauma or help them settle in. Their records show their real names."

"What about the other two? Have they said anything?"

"Not a word. They are a tight group. They've been in foster care for three years now and only have each other. They maintain they didn't go to the beach that night and don't know why Jimmy would run."

"Can I speak to them?"

"Of course, but it will have to wait until tomorrow. Some of our youth workers took a group of them to the city today, a special outing to Playland. They've been through a lot in the last couple of weeks. We want them to have a fun day before school starts up and take their mind off Jimmy."

"Thank you, Eugene. I will drop by tomorrow, then."

"OK, I will let them know."

Julie returns to the station and catches Brooks about to leave his office.

"Hello, sir, is this a bad time? I know it's late, but you told me to check in?"

"Sure, Morneau, what do you have?"

"Well, sir, I spoke to one of the workers at the youth home. It's possible a couple of the kids may know something. One of them coincidentally ran away the day after the assault and they have not been able to locate him."

"He ran away?" Brooks says. "Did they report it?"

"Apparently the tribal police have been working with the home to find him. We were notified and have been active in the search, but he hasn't turned up. I believe Marks was liaising with tribal, but we had no reason to make the connection until now."

"When are you going to interview them?"

"I will follow up with them in the morning," Julie says. "They are on some outing to the city at present."

"OK, Morneau, I will attend with you."

"Sure. Did you get an update on the victim, sir?"

"Not yet. I'm working on it. I'll talk to you tomorrow."

"OK, Sergeant. I'll see you in the morning."

Ramsey Community Centre

At seven o'clock on Sunday evening, Ramsey Community Centre is filled to capacity. Almost one hundred seething souls have turned out to share their perspectives on the issues of the day. They are business owners, housewives, hipsters, self-proclaimed nationalists and curious troublemakers. While the gathering might look random, it is anything but. Some have been strategically placed to sway sentiment and grind the axe.

Robert Groomer observes the crowd from the back of the room, carefully sketching out his front page for the morning. He draws a line down the centre of his paper with two headings: "Concerned Citizen" and "Maniac."

Tonight's town hall is the design of Mayor Connie Beck in response to a barrage of phone calls to her office and local police looking for details on the Nora Beach assault. Tensions are escalating thanks to amped-up media chatter on radio talk shows about conspiracy theories and vigilante rhetoric of every type and persuasion. A reality that seems lost on Ramsey's fine mayor.

The sixty-year-old Ramsey-born, locally educated mayor is up for reelection in two months and could not pass up an opportunity to spew more cliché-ridden sentiment. One wouldn't call the mayor trite, exactly, but her intentions lack a certain vigor of effort required to justify her persuasion. Her inability to thoroughly gauge the atmosphere of the room soon becomes apparent, as she finds herself overwhelmed by the crowd.

A young woman steps up to the microphone. "Good evening, Mayor Beck. How are you this evening?"

"I'm just fine, dear. How are those lovely twins of yours?"

"They are just fine, Mayor, thanks for asking. Mayor, I think the police should be cracking down on drifters around Nora Beach. I mean, it's a known fact that the shelter attracts crime to the area, and homeless people who can't get a bed there pitch anywhere. It's getting so I don't want to walk Nora Beach by myself anymore. There's always an out of towner sleeping on the beach, getting into trouble. I'm full of sympathy for those people, God bless them, but you know, Mayor, sometimes they're on drugs. Every year, they make their way from the city. Maybe the shelter should be moved to a more industrial area."

"I hear what you're saying, Marcie. Thank you."

A senior man takes to the second mic. "Mayor, I noticed a police car at Shannon House today. Is that where the trouble is coming from? It wouldn't be the first time."

"No, Jeffery, I didn't hear anything about that. That could be an entirely different matter. It's important not to speculate."

A large man in a camouflage coat takes the senior's place at microphone two. "Some of those kids from the reserve have been around a lot since the surf's been up. Have the police questioned them? Maybe tribal should be helping out here?"

"Well now, sir, Nora Beach is for everyone to enjoy, you know that. The mere presence of First Nations doesn't mean they're up to no good. And yes, tribal police are also helping us with this matter."

Sam Roche, owner of the local surf shop steps up.

"Hello, Mayor, do we even know who this guy is? What tribe is he from?"

"I don't, sir, but I am going to let Councillor Steves answer that."

Councillor Steves steps up to the mayor's microphone.

"No, we don't have that information yet," he says. "I have been getting updates from Ramsey PD and I understand some inquiries have been made into the man's status and location, so we are hopeful that word is getting out and someone will come forward. According to the paper, his name is Daiji, but there is no known family yet."

One of the surfers approaches the microphone.

"Yes, his name is Daiji. He is a First Nations man—a kind, decent man. He was on a spiritual journey to help and serve others with his wisdom and healing. He was travelling. He was at home on the beach. He was at home with himself. He was a friend to everyone. He didn't ask for the teepee, but we built him one anyway. Whoever did this deserves to be punished. We should focus on solving the crime, this violent act, instead of condemning the victim."

A comment is hurled from the back of the room. "His wisdom and healing aren't helping him now."

Steves ignores the grumbling from the crowd. "Thank you. We are hoping to learn more about this man's family in the coming days."

Christopher Stamer, a well-known activist in the community and a thorn in the mayor's side, takes his turn at the microphone. "Good evening, Mayor Beck. Thank you for joining us."

"Good evening, Christopher," she says.

"Mayor, maybe this would be a good time to discuss your affordable housing plan. You have a little time left. Are you any closer to meeting your goals?"

Against his better judgment, Stamer, a fifty-five-year-old lawyer, recently tossed his hat into the political arena, a move he resisted for years despite pressure from his colleagues. Stamer was motivated by a controversial action taken by the city of Vancouver to destroy entire communities in the city's downtown to build an extensive freeway system—a move he declared was a dangerous trend targeting vulnerable minority communities. Stamer's outrage with the decision to bulldoze Hogan's Alley, a Black Canadian community, was the tipping point and he announced his intention to run.

In a passionate speech on the lower east side, surrounded by press and activists, Stamer vowed he would no longer stand on the sidelines. He gave an explosive rant expressing frustration with a system strategically designed to benefit the privileged and promised to expose injustice at all costs.

"Well, thank you, Christopher for joining us," the mayor says. "I see you took the time to campaign tonight?"

Other members of the crowd take advantage of the lead-in and jump at the opportunity.

"It's true, Mayor, this town is in crisis! People can't afford to pay rent. Pretty soon we'll all be camped on the beach."

"Chris has a point, Mayor. We applied for a shelter expansion three years ago and there has been very little in the way of commitment from your office."

"I understand your frustration," Mayor Beck replies. "I have shared all of your concerns about housing with the province, but it's out of my hands."

The familiar comment receives moans and eye rolls, but then an angry voice from the back of the room booms: "We wouldn't need a shelter if the feds would stop opening our door to every drug dealer and asylum seeker on the planet!"

A surfer in the crowd steps to an open mic to respond. "Maybe we should cage them and ship them back. You work for UPS, Reg, don't ya?"

Members of the crowd who know Reg clearly become uncomfortable with the brave rebuttal and bow their heads, bracing for the reaction.

Reg takes a step toward the slight surfer. "Maybe you should be sent somewhere, too, you fucking hippie. In case you didn't know, you dimwit, it's illegal to build a teepee on the beach."

Although he's clearly unprepared for the focused rage, the young man nervously stands his ground. Stamer gets between them and attempts to deescalate.

"OK now, Reg, we know you're frustrated. We all are. That's why we're here tonight. It's important to talk it out, but we don't need any threats."

The mayor attempts to rein in the argument. She hustles a few council members to the front of the room to help navigate the microphones.

"OK, OK, everyone, we're getting off topic just a bit," she says. "We can't cover every social issue and political opinion in the room. We are here to discuss safety and perhaps gather some information about the victim of this assault. Can we keep this to a friendly discussion about safety, please?"

Groomer steps outside, lights a cigarette, and pushes a quarter into the payphone.

"Ramsey Police Department. Sadie speaking."

"This is Robert Groomer from the Chronicle. I'm attending the town hall at the community centre tonight and I was asked to call in if things amped up. Well, you could say it's getting a little warm in there."

"What do you mean exactly, Robert? What's happening over there?"

"I have nothing else to say, Sadie. Just a heads up. I'm sure the good mayor will handle it. Do with it what you will. Goodnight."

Groomer stamps out his cigarette butt and walks back inside.

Daiji

"W*ell, I come from Alabama with my banjo on my knee, and I'm going to Louisiana my own true love for to see. It rained all night the day I left, the weather it was dry. The sun so hot I froze to death—Susanna, don't you cry...*"

The sun breaks through the clouds, creating a dazzling sparkle on the surface of Rubin Bay. A warm breeze creates gentle ripples on the liquid mirror that rocks the canoe in a psychedelic lull. Daiji sings and paddles his way around the calm inlet.

He knows the waters of Rubin. It's a beautiful place to explore, with many beaches and reminders of the past. His ancestors trod these shores before and he knows where to find the secret traces of lives once lived. He used to spend hours as a boy beachcombing and foraging in the forest, enjoying a nostalgic step back in time. He became so immersed in his adventures, he would barely make it home before dark.

Daiji watches the sky. The afternoon wind can whip up without warning, bringing the waves to frightening heights. A sudden change may require a demanding dance with the waves or an unexpected return to shore.

But no decisions are needed now. Today, the water quietly reflects the beauty of the blue and white sky. All he has to do is float.

Chelsey Health Centre

Physiotherapist, Jason Langley sits quietly at the bedside of his new patient. It's hard to determine his age—mid-forties, maybe older? Except for the yellow and purple bruises, his skin is brown and smooth. His head is bandaged from the surgery to release the swelling in his brain. There are bruises on his arms and his torso is wrapped to support multiple broken ribs.

Jason examines Daiji for some sign of awareness. His skin is perfect, with no sign of breakdown. Respiration is good, better than good. Jason takes the patient's arm carefully and tests movement. He bends it at the elbow and gently raises it, then lowers it. Range is normal and movement is smooth.

He repeats the same on the other side. Then his legs. They appear to be in good shape. Jason touches reflex points on the man's foot, hoping for some kind of response. Nothing. He completes a full assessment, quietly speaking to the patient as he bends, stretches, and taps his compact body. Despite his severe injuries, he has a peaceful countenance.

"It can't be too bad of a place, wherever you are. It seems to be working for you," Jason says.

A soft light breaks through the blinds, and Jason hums an old song he used to sing with his mother when he was just a boy. He chuckles to himself as he recognizes his nostalgia. Where did that come from?

His patient's breathing is smooth, quiet, almost meditative. Jason smiles at the face below him.

"It's a rainy evening, Daiji. Summer is coming to an end, I'm afraid, but there's something peaceful about the rain, don't you think?"

He senses a presence. He leans closer to him and whispers, "You are with me, aren't you, Daiji?"

An Emergency Meeting at Ramsey PD

Anthony Brooks leads a last-minute meeting at the station. "OK, everyone, things are ramping up. We need to update you on what we have learned to this point."

The sergeant is interrupted by Sadie, who softly relays a message. Brooks looks out into the waiting room to see his ten a.m. appointment. A small group of First Nations elders have come forward and may be able to offer some information on the victim.

"OK, I'll be with them as soon as I'm done here. Twenty minutes, tops. Thank you, Sadie."

Brooks begins again, focusing on the officers in front of him. "I take it you've all seen the news this morning. Groomer captured quite the scene at the community centre last night. It seems discussions became rather heated. The meeting was called off an hour after it started. There were a few patriots in attendance last night who decided to throw some chairs around after offending everyone with their racist bullshit. They were taken into custody and are standing before a judge this afternoon.

"Hannah and Clarke didn't get a whole lot from them last night, but we will be keeping a close eye on their whereabouts. It seems they don't like outsiders lingering on the beach. I need someone to check in with the mayor. Apparently she was rushed out of there and will certainly have opinions on the matter. I think we should also pay a visit to Christopher Stamer, who was particularly vocal last night. He seems to have an uncanny ability to irritate his opponents. Pick his brain. He may be able to offer some insight into who could hate this guy enough to do this.

"Morneau and I are following up with some youth at Shannon House who may know something. Questions?"

"Do we have any updates on the victim?" asks Constable Clarke.

"He's still not conscious, but we may know more this afternoon. It seems there are a few folks from Nuu-chah-nulth who are waiting to speak. OK, if there is anything else, please relay it to Hannah. That's it for now. Morneau, come with me."

Julie rushes to the front to catch up with Brooks, who is already headed to the waiting area.

"Did they say they know him?" she asks.

"Well, they haven't said anything yet, but I appreciate your enthusiasm. They may want to hear a little about what this guy has been doing for the last few weeks, so I am counting on you to help with that part."

"I'll do what I can, sir."

The officers invite the group into Brooks's office.

"Good morning, gentlemen and lady," Brooks says. "Thank you for coming in. I am Sergeant Anthony Brooks and this is Constable Julie Morneau."

They shake hands. An Indigenous man of approximately sixty-five years makes the introductions.

"Good morning officers," he says. "My name is Anton Williams from Hupacasath Nation. These are Rudy Young and Barbara Brown. We are members of the Nuu-chah-nulth Traditional Healers Council, and based on the photo we have seen on the news, we believe we may know the individual who was assaulted on the beach."

"It's a pleasure to meet you. We are eager to hear what you have to say," says Brooks. "Please take a seat." He retrieves a file from his desk and takes out a photo. "You mean this man?"

The three lean forward to look closely at the picture of Daiji. Barbara smiles and bows her head in obvious recognition.

"That is him. I'm sure of it. He comes from Tseshaht First Nations near the Mackana Valley. I know him well. He was on an important journey."

"Oh really? What journey was that?" asks Brooks.

"You see, officer, part of the mandate of our council is to promote and educate our people on traditional healing practices," says Anton. "Generations of our people have been stripped of their culture. So much has been lost. We find ourselves in the unfortunate situation of having to reeducate our children about who they are and where they come from. We have to teach them a way of being that no longer comes naturally to them.

"Daiji was committed to this task. He believed the time has come for a call to action. We cannot change the past, but Daiji felt that to truly lead future generations of our people, we have to empower them through our cultural practices and traditions. He wanted to teach a holistic and balanced approach to life and wellness. Daiji is a gifted healer. All people, especially the youth, have much to learn from him."

"He sounds like a wonderful man, and we are doing everything we can to find out what happened here. Do you happen to know his last name?" asks Brooks.

Barbara speaks softly. "Daiji is his medicine name. His original name is Josef Brown."

Barbara is a fifty-five-year-old elder from Mackana Valley. Her long black hair is held in place with a symbolic headband. Her green eyes sparkle in a face of smooth brown skin and her soft smile extends to her high cheekbones.

"Daiji is my cousin," says Barbara. "I would like to see him. Can he speak?"

"All we know at this point is that Daiji is fighting hard to be well. He was given a bed at the health centre in Chelsey, where professionals are working to help him recover. He has a brain injury and has been in a coma for a couple of weeks now, but we remain hopeful."

"What happened to him?"

"We are still trying to piece that together. His injuries could have come from a direct assault, or he may have been hit by some object. It's not clear and there are no witnesses that we know of. We are following up on some leads today and hoping to learn more about what happened to Daiji.

"Constable Morneau was familiar with Daiji and she may be able to tell you a little more. In the meantime, we would be happy to take you to the hospital where he's being treated. We obviously need to speak with him as well. Sergeant Hannah will arrange that for you and accompany you on the trip."

"I can tell you that Daiji did make a small circle of friends here in Ramsey," says Julie. "Some of the surfers spend hours on the beach and are well-acquainted with him. They built him a small shelter. He enjoyed it there and spent time talking with them and telling stories. He really is a healer."

"Yes, Daiji spent a lot of time on the water. It was where he found his peace," says Barbara.

"That explains a lot," says Julie. "I do believe he was fulfilling his journey. I am very sorry it was interrupted in such a violent, senseless way. We will get to the bottom of this. I do know from hospital staff that he is fighting hard and receiving quality care."

Barbara bows her head. Anton takes her hand and says, "He is doing what he needs to do. You know Daiji. He takes his time."

The three elders stand. Anton passes Brooks his card. "This is how you can reach us. When can we expect to go to Chelsey?"

"We will set that up this afternoon and shoot for a departure in the next day or two. Someone will call you with the details this evening."

"Thank you, officers."

"Thank you for coming in."

Chelsey Health Centre

Monday morning is abuzz at Chelsey Health Centre. Sandra Braxton, the nurse manager for the fourth floor tops up her second cup of dark roast coffee before opening the morning report. Weekend reports are rife with the unexpected. An unknown relative makes an impromptu visit, someone misses their medication, a locked unit is suddenly unlocked. Mr. Lancaster in 407 fell and broke his hip on a late-night trip to the bathroom.

Sandra sighs. "Oh, poor soul."

Finally, the bed in 424B, once reserved for respite support, has a new occupant from out of town named Daiji. He is unresponsive but stable. Nasogastric tube and soft rehab required. She is surprised by the few details and many unknowns. Sandra decides to check in on this Daiji. As she makes her way down Corridor B, she meets Cindy Rogers, who is finishing up a night shift. Cindy has never been a fan of night shift and seldom misses an opportunity to say so. She locks a supply room door and smiles at Sandra.

"Good morning," says Cindy.

Sandra pulls out of her thoughts and responds. "Pardon me?"

Cindy laughs. "I said good morning, Sandra."

"Oh!" Sandra chuckles, shocked that Cindy bothered to make the effort, never mind wear a smile.

"Good morning, Cindy. How was your weekend?"

Cindy's smile widens. "Just lovely."

"Lovely? Good, good, glad to hear it. Enjoy your days off," says Sandra.

"I will, thanks. Have a good day," says Cindy.

Sandra arrives at 424B, a room smaller than most in the wing. Its very shape says it was an afterthought, a final attempt to maximize space in an overburdened system. Nevertheless, the room has a quiet charm, with a bed, a half bath, and a window that faces the north end of Chelsey Forest. This morning, its sage green walls are softly lit to accommodate the brain-injured Daiji. At his bedside sits a visitor, Joanie Freeman. Joanie is a darling eighty-five-year-old with worsening COPD and moderate dementia, but she always wears a smile.

"Joanie, what are you doing here?" Sandra asks.

"Shh, he's sleeping," says Joanie. "He looks so peaceful."

Sandra focuses on Daiji. "Good morning, Daiji." He does look peaceful, almost smiling.

Sandra immediately checks the chart at the foot of Daiji's bed. It reads the same as her admission. Traumatic brain injury: Glasgow coma scale score is eleven. "OK, Daiji, we need to move that number."

Joanie looks at her quizzically. "What's his name, dear?"

"It's Daiji," says Sandra.

Joanie smiles. "That's nice," she says.

"Yes, it is, Joanie. Where he comes from, it likely means something special."

"Perhaps he will tell us," says Joanie.

"Yes, perhaps he will," says Sandra.

Shannon House

Brooks and Julie sit in the conference room in Shannon House, waiting to question thirteen-year-old Jonathan Richards and ten-year-old Lisa Roberts, half-siblings through a mutual mother. Both officers understand the delicacy of the meeting. These children each have their own particular history with the police. They know these meetings often bring upheaval to their already chaotic lives. Bags will be packed, goodbyes said, and what's left is a distasteful diet of false hope. These children have learned that the truth offers neither freedom nor beauty. It's best to remain silent.

The two children enter the room with Eugene, as if being led to their deaths. Lisa is petite for a ten-year-old. Her smooth brown hair hangs loose to her shoulders. She clings to her brother's hand with her head down. She takes quick glimpses at the officers, as if looking too closely is a trap. She and her brother are of Indigenous origin, and like most children at Shannon House, have lived a thousand lives in little more than a decade. Lisa fidgets and immediately reaches for the colouring materials set out for her on the table. Jonathan is stoic. His face offers little evidence of childhood. He looks closed off, empty, and tired.

"Hello," says Brooks. He extends his hand to Jonathan, who obliges.

"Hello," Jonathan says bluntly.

Lisa throws them a look and hurriedly continues to colour in a unicorn.

"I'm Sergeant Brooks and this is Constable Morneau. Thank you for joining us, Jonathan. And is this Lisa?" Brooks asks.

Lisa takes another quick glimpse and nods.

"So, I understand you have already talked to the police. Is that right?" Brooks says.

"Yes," says Jonathan.

"We don't know where Jimmy is," says Lisa, who continues to colour.

"Jimmy. Right, that's your older brother?"

Lisa nods without taking her eyes off her task.

"Yes, we heard he ran away. Did he tell you where he was going?"

They both shake their heads.

Brooks focuses in on a tense-looking Jonathan. "Any idea why he would just run off like that?"

Jonathan shakes his head again.

"He doesn't like it here," says Lisa. "He says they are going to take him away again."

This catches Jonathan off guard. He shoots his sister a look, but Lisa is oblivious to any fallout from her comment and continues to colour another picture.

Jonathan continues where Lisa left off. "He always says that. We didn't know he was leaving."

"The night before he left, you guys were late coming in. Where were you that night?" asks Brooks.

Jonathan gives a deep, annoyed sigh. "We already told the other police officer. We were at the park, down the street."

"Oh, I see. The park," says Brooks. He directs his attention to Lisa. "Were you near the beach at all?"

Lisa lifts her eyes and looks at her brother. The colouring has stopped.

"No," she says.

Jonathan takes a direct approach. “We don’t know what happened to that guy, if that’s what you’re getting at.”

“Oh, you heard about that, huh? What did you hear?”

Jonathan jumps in before his sister can respond. “The other officer asked if we heard anything about the guy who was beat up on the beach, but we were at the park that night.”

Lisa looks at her brother, drops her head, and concentrates on her picture.

“What did Jimmy say about it?” Brooks asks.

“Jimmy didn’t say anything about it,” says Jonathan. “He was at the park too.”

Brook softens. “OK, OK. I’m not trying to upset you, Jonathan. If I am, then I apologize for that. You see, Constable Morneau and I are looking for some clues, some answers. This man, Daiji is his name, is a good man. He’s a healer, you know.”

“What do you mean, a healer?” asks Jonathan.

Lisa freezes, holding her turquoise blue crayon, her eyes fixed on Brooks.

“Well, he is Indigenous like you. He came from the Tseshaht Nation. Do you know where that is?”

Both children shake their heads.

“He’s an elder and a healer, and he was traveling in the area to teach people about Indigenous traditions. He was living on the beach. Did you know that?”

“No,” says Lisa.

Brooks and Julie share a look.

“He has some family who are worried about him,” Brooks says. “They’re going to see him today.”

“Is he going to be OK?” asks Jonathan.

“Well, we don’t know yet, unfortunately,” says Brooks. “We will find out more today. We are really hoping he will be awake soon so he can tell us what happened.”

Jonathan looks overwhelmed with thought. He gives a distracted nod. Julie senses the weight on his shoulders and leans in.

"We thought you might have seen something because you live close to the beach—an accident or smoke, anything that might help us."

Jonathan likes her kind face.

"No, we don't know anything," Lisa says in a sing-song response that sounds rehearsed, her head down.

"Well, Constable Morneau is going to give you her card, and if you think of anything, you ask Eugene to give us a call, OK?"

Jonathan takes the card. "OK," he says.

Brooks and Julie leave Shannon House together.

"You can't push these kids too hard. They're smart, they know what we're looking for. Did you see that thirteen-year-old? He knows the system," Brooks says.

"They know something," says Julie. "They may not know where their brother went, but they know why."

"One step at a time," says Brooks. "One step at a time."

Chelsey Health Centre

Jason Langley's first stop of the morning is to see his newest patient in 424B. The physiotherapist moves Daiji's arms and hands, talking to him as he flexes each limb and sets them down again.

"Can you hear me, Daiji?" he asks. He lightly presses Daiji's palm. His voice is low and calm. "I would like you to let me know if you are."

Jason receives a small squeeze back from his patient.

"That's it, thank you, Daiji. Little steps, that's what we need. You have all the time in the world." Jason hums as he works.

A bubbly Sandra Braxton appears, giggling. "Well, you seem happy this morning. What's the tune you're humming?"

"Oh, hi Sandra."

"Well, what was it?"

"What's what?" asks Jason.

"The tune you were humming."

"Oh." Jason laughs. "I'm not entirely sure. Daiji seems to bring it out in me."

"How's he looking?"

Sandra has been quietly observing the process from the doorway.

She knows the therapist's reputation with the severely injured. "Jason of Rehabeth" did not come by his title merely due to his striking good looks and goatee. He is known by nurses and therapists in rehab for his miracles with supposedly doomed patients.

Jason once worked with a young man named Miguel who was injured in a skiing accident that resulted in several broken vertebrae and countless internal injuries. Doctors told him he would have to change his lifestyle and give up the physical pursuits he enjoyed so much, and that he would be lucky to walk again.

Miguel's mental state quickly began to deteriorate. Life as he knew it was over. Within two months, his treatment for depression was taking priority over his physical injuries. He was on suicide watch and being spoon-fed. Necessary surgeries were postponed because Miguel's mental health seriously jeopardized their success. Jason spent numerous hours working with Miguel, empowering him to focus, heal, and work toward recovery. One year later, Miguel was back on his skis.

Miguel's family attributed his remarkable recovery to Jason's holistic coaching, reminding his patient that the body has the power to heal, but often the mind gets in the way. This comment brought Jason criticism from management, who accused him of creating false hope among medically dependent patients who, in some minds, needed professional encouragement to adapt. Nevertheless, his endless commitment to his work and the success of his patients could not be denied.

"He has some small motor commands that seem intentional, but nothing verbal. No eye opening yet," says Jason.

Sandra smiles. "Yet."

"His Glasgow coma score is eleven. There's hope in that number. His palms and skin feel good. He's with us, but his mind is somewhere else. Wherever he is, he's working hard."

"Well, that's quite possible," says Sandra.

"What do you mean?" asks Jason.

"Some nations on the coast take a holistic approach to trauma," says Sandra. "It's not just the physical injury that needs to be healed. There's a lot of spiritual work that goes into recovery to restore balance. But you understand this already, Jason."

"Yes, of course. But you think he's a shaman, then?"

"Let's hope so," says Sandra. "He seems to be having a positive effect around here."

Jason and Sandra are interrupted by a voice from the hallway.

"Can I come in?"

"Case in point," says Sandra. "What is it, Joanie?"

"Just checking on my neighbor. Is he awake yet?"

"No, not yet, Joanie, and we really don't know if that will happen," says Sandra.

"It will happen," says Joanie. She takes the chair next to Daiji's bed.

"Do you like sitting with Daiji?" asks Jason.

"Yes. I hope that's ok. I think he wants me here."

"That's fine, Joanie. Company is good for him," says Jason.

Joanie looks around the room. "It's peaceful here," she says.

"I understand," says Jason.

Sandra and Jason leave the room as Joanie holds the hand of the newest patient and begins to hum.

Daiji

"W*ell, I had a dream the other night when everything was still. I dreamed that I saw Susanna dear a-coming down the hill...*"

A moving shadow on the starboard side breaks Daiji from his reverie. He looks to the sky, but then the sound of pressured air pulls his gaze below. A curious seal taking a look? Daiji feels a vibration as his canoe is nudged to the left. Not a seal—it feels like something else.

He places his paddle across the canoe, listening closely to the creaking depths below. He braces himself, barely breathing.

A large mammal breaks the surface on the port side. Water shoots up ten feet in front of him. That's no seal!

Daiji laughs and howls with delight. Oh, no, it's too close! He grabs the side of the boat, clutching the paddle on the left as a six-ton orca breaches in his path, crashes back to the surface, and showers him in its wake.

Daiji swallows water. Another breach!

He dips his paddle in the water and allows his body to sway with the swell, like his father showed him years ago. He must not resist the force. The displaced water rolls the boat deeply to the left. Daiji bends his back toward the surface, almost lying in the water. He coughs out seawater and braces himself again.

There are two of them. Two massive orcas moving fast.

Visitors

Sergeant Hannah arrives with the elders at Four North and are greeted by Sandra, the floor manager.

"Good day, I heard you were coming," she says. "My name is Sandra."

"Hello, I'm Sergeant Michael Hannah and these are Anton, Barbara, and Rudy—friends of your patient Daiji."

"It's a pleasure to meet you all," says Sandra. "I'm so glad he'll have visitors. We have become very fond of Daiji. Please come this way."

Sandra fills the visitors in on Daiji's status as they walk. "He's not yet responding to vocal commands, but it doesn't mean he can't hear you. We like to think he is aware of our presence."

"Yes, we understand," says Barbara.

Daiji lies peacefully in his bed. Most of the bruising has healed and his face looks peaceful, but far away. He wears a slight smile. The room is quiet. Barbara approaches his side and softly lays his hand in hers. She leans in close, speaking softly in their native language.

The other two elders take position on either side, heads bowed, eyes closed. Barbara's words are soft and sound like a prayer. Daiji remains still.

The three elders stay with Daiji for several hours before returning to Sandra, who is sitting in an office with Sergeant Hannah.

"How was your visit?" asks Sandra.

"Very good. I can sense his presence," says Barbara. "You have done a good job of healing his physical wounds. Now he must heal his spirit. Daiji is healing from the inside. We will be back tomorrow."

Sergeant Hannah stands and thanks Sandra, and the visitors depart.

Robbie

"You are just a savage. Savages can't learn anything. You are nothing."

Robbie is standing in front of his class with his pants down.

"Savages must be taught."

Supervisor Klint straps him once, twice, three times. Robbie wants to move away from the pain and the slash of the strap, but he can't. Every time he jumps or moves, it means five more whippings. His teacher has chosen to leave the room and drink tea while the students were forced to stay. Supervisor Klint wants to teach them all an important lesson today.

"You will learn, Robbie." Klint grunts from the strain of winding his arm high in the air and crashes the strap down across Robbie's back and buttocks.

Robbie cries. His classmates are silent. Some cover their eyes. The girls cringe with every blow of the thick leather strap and the boys are frozen at their desks, terrified they will be next. The lunch bell rings. The students and Klint leave the room. They leave Robbie there alone, pants down, buckled over on the floor.

Robbie wants to die right there on the spot. At least then, he won't feel this fear anymore. Maybe he will be buried next to Edward in the back among all the trees. Maybe his family will visit his grave and remember him as a baby boy. Yes, that would be better.

He's sent to bed without supper, shackled to the bed posts to prevent him from getting up, even to use the bathroom. His pyjama pants are soaked in urine, but he's forced to lie on his burning back, crying and hungry, thinking about his nothingness and the fact that he's a savage. He cries until he's too exhausted to make another sound. His head feels heavy and hot.

Then a voice he recognizes whispers in his ear.

"We're getting out of here. I'm getting us out."

Jonathan Richards starts awake in his bed. His forehead is moist and his face damp from tears. His bedding lies in a crumpled heap on the floor, and he feels out of breath. He remembers where he is and wipes the tears from his eyes.

They got out. RJ got them out but now he's alone. He misses his brother. They change towns, homes, and names, but nothing works. They're always running.

He wishes they could stop running.

Ramsey Police Department

Sergeant Brooks and Julie meet in Brooks's office to discuss next steps in the assault when Clarke interrupts.

"We just had a report from Shannon House," he says. "Someone defaced their monument. The word 'Shannon' was crossed out and 'juvie' was sprayed over it. The side of the building was sprayed in red paint reading 'home of the guilty.'"

Brooks drops his head. "No more interviews at Shannon House. Any other questioning in this case will have to be done here—youth, mayor, it doesn't matter. Bring them in for their own safety. Constable Morneau, can you make sure everyone understands this?"

"Of course. I'll send out a memo to everyone."

"Thanks, Clarke," says Brooks.

"Someone has been watching where we're going, who we're talking to," says Julie.

"So it seems," says Brooks.

"Clarke says the mayor also received a threat about allowing immigrants in, as if she controls that," says Julie.

"They don't care. These people think they can scare those with the most influence in town into seeing their side of things, so the mayor is a target."

Brooks punches numbers into his phone and gives a direct order. “Clarke, get an eye on the mayor. She could be a target if things amp up here.”

“Will do, sir. Constable Morneau has a call on line two.”

Brooks hands Julie the phone. She listens intently for several moments throwing Brooks a look of concern. “OK, sure. Yes, we’ll be here.” She looks at Brooks. “It’s the kid, Jonathan. He wants to talk. Eugene is bringing him in the morning.”

Chelsey Health Centre

Jason agreed to a Saturday shift to greet Daiji's visitors. The elders have already gathered at his bedside. The eldest of the three, Rudy, stands at Daiji's head. He holds a sachet of sweetgrass in his hands. Barbara sits in a chair at Daiji's feet and Anton is at his right, with his hands touching Daiji's chest.

They softly chant with eyes closed. Barbara holds a wooden carving in her hand that her cousin gave her years ago.

Daiji continues to lie silently in a peaceful stillness. There is a slight smell of sweetgrass in the room. Every once in a while, they break and leave the room, sip water, and discuss his progress, only to return to him again.

Daiji

Daiji looks at the widening inlet ahead of him, the gateway from Rubin Bay to the vast ocean. It's time for the whales to move out. They were simply following their path, and he was in the way. He sighs in deep relief, grateful for the added distance as the two playful giants find their way to the ocean. He decides it's time to change direction. It's getting late, the wind is picking up, and he's needed at home.

Daiji heads back to shore.

A Confession

Jonathan Richards is escorted to a small interview room. Brooks and Julie meet him there. The young boy walks with the weight of the world on his shoulders.

"Nice to see you again, Jonathan. Please take a seat," says Brooks.

He motions to a chair at the table, where Julie is already seated. Jonathan looks timidly at the constable and gives a slight smile as he sits.

"I understand you want to speak with us, Jonathan," she says.

"Yes," he says.

Julie notices he is holding something, a small carving of some kind that he rubs between his fingers.

"Well, we are very glad to see you. What's on your mind?" she asks.

"I know what happened to the man on the beach," he says.

"Really? What do you know?" asks Brooks.

Jonathan notices a tape recorder has been turned on.

"I have to tape this, Jonathan," says Brooks. "This is important."

Jonathan nods. "I know the man. Daiji. We were visiting him that night. It was an accident."

"Who was visiting him, Jonathan?"

"Me and Lisa. But Lisa doesn't know anything. She was just there, that's all."

"OK, OK, that's fine, Jonathan. Continue."

"We visited the medicine man a couple of times. He was living in the teepee the surfers made. He would give us things like carvings and tell us stories about his people and our people. We liked going there."

"How many times did you see him?"

"Um, twice. That's all. The last time we saw him, he had a fire burning. There was a hole in the top of the hut for the smoke. He was showing us the animal carvings he made and telling us stories about his family."

"Well, it sounds like it started off as a good visit," says Julie.

Jonathan nods. "Yes, it did."

"What happened next?" asks Brooks.

"Then he asked about our family. He wanted to know where we lived."

"I see," says Brooks. "He asked about your family."

"We don't like answering those questions. Everyone asks those questions. Why won't people just leave us alone?"

"People ask those questions because it's a way to get to know you better," Brooks says.

"Not for us. When people ask us those questions, they want to trap us. They want to take us away, find out what we're doing wrong, even though we aren't doing anything wrong. 'Where are your parents? Why aren't you with them? Where do you live now? Do you like it there? Does everyone get along?' The more we answer those questions, the more we have to move. We are together now."

"You mean, you and Lisa are together," Brooks says.

"Yes, and Jimmy. But Jimmy left. Jimmy was with us, and he left."

"Why do you think he left?"

"I told you I don't know."

"Has Jimmy met Daiji?"

"No. Just me and Lisa."

"Jonathan, we understand. You get scared when someone asks those questions because of what you have experienced in the past."

Jonathan nods.

"What happened then, Jonathan, after the questions?" asks Brooks.

"I stood up and told Lisa we were leaving, but Daiji stood up too and tried to stop me. He put his hand on my shoulder."

"Did he hurt you or threaten you, Jonathan?"

"No, no," says Jonathan. "He was trying to calm me down. He was saying he was sorry."

Jonathan drops his head and begins to cry.

"It's OK, Jonathan," says Julie softly.

"Jonathan," says Brooks. "I want you to know that I think you are very brave to come here today to tell us what happened. I believe it will help you in the long run. I need you to tell me what you did to Daiji when he tried to calm you down."

Jonathan looks up and quickly wipes away the escaping tears. "I punched him."

"Where did you punch him?" asks Brooks.

Jonathan pauses and closes his eyes, as if he can't believe his own words. "I punched him in the face and then I kicked him."

"How many times did you punch and kick him, Jonathan?"

"I don't know. A lot." He looks away and fidgets in his chair.

"More than twice?" asks Brooks.

"Yes, more than that." He stares straight ahead, expressionless.

Julie closes her eyes, trying not to imagine the kind, quiet man in the grips of such a violent attack.

"OK, Jonathan. I need you to stay with us," Brooks says. "We have to get these details. How did the teepee collapse?"

"I'm not sure," he says. "I was trying to get Lisa out and it just collapsed."

Brooks and Julie share a look.

"What do you mean, you were trying to get Lisa out?" Brooks says. "You were kicking and punching Daiji, and then you were trying to get Lisa out?"

Jonathan silently searches his mind for the answer.

Brooks presses on. "Do you know how the teepee collapsed, Jonathan?"

"I don't remember anything else," Jonathan says, fighting back his tears.

"We are almost done, Jonathan. We have to get this right. Is it your statement that you were standing up when Daiji touched your shoulder to calm you down? Then you punched and kicked him, and he was still standing?"

"No, he fell down," says Jonathan.

"How did he fall?" asks Brooks.

"I think he knocked the teepee down when he fell."

"You think, but you're not sure?"

"I don't know," Jonathan says, on the verge of tears.

Brooks leans in and looks directly at Jonathan. "The teepee the surfers built was very strong. I'm surprised it just collapsed like that."

Jonathan holds Brooks's gaze and nods.

"The canvas was cut into shreds, like a knife was used. Did you cut it?"

"No. I don't know about that."

"Jonathan, are you covering for your brother?"

Jonathan jumps to his feet and shouts at Brooks. "I did this! It was me."

Julie is taken by surprise at the unexpected eruption from the shy boy. She stands and touches him lightly.

"OK, Jonathan, it's OK. Sergeant Brooks has to ask hard questions to make sure he has the right person. We believe you."

"Jonathan, I'm not trying to upset you. I have to be tough with these questions or I'm not doing my job. Is there anything else you remember?" Brooks asks.

Jonathan sits back down and takes a deep breath.

"I get in a fog sometimes when I get scared. It's like a brain fuzz. It's scary and I have to fight my way out. I don't really know what I'm doing.

"Daiji fell and the teepee started to come apart. One of the logs came loose and hit him in the head. I thought we were all going to die, so I grabbed Lisa and we ran out."

"You left Daiji in there?"

"I didn't know it was going to catch on fire. We didn't mean for it to happen."

"Who didn't mean for it to happen?"

"I didn't mean for it to happen."

"Jonathan, Daiji was outside the teepee."

Jonathan looks at Brooks, confused. "He was?"

"Yes, he was. In fact, it looks like he was dragged outside. Do you know who dragged him outside?"

"No, I don't," Jonathan says. He looks at his hands. "I don't know how that happened."

"Did you hurt your hands, Jonathan?" Julie asks, looking at his smooth, unmarked hands.

"They're all better now," he says.

"Jonathan, this brain fog—have you ever told anyone about it or looked for help for this?"

"No."

Brooks stands. "Jonathan, we're glad you came in and shared this story with us. We have to talk to Eugene for a moment. Would you wait here for us, please? We'll be right back, OK?"

Jonathan nods.

"Constable Morneau, can you come with me, please?"

The two officers step outside.

"He's covering," says Brooks.

Julie shakes her head. "Poor kid. Why, why would he cover for his brother?"

"He's probably the closest the kid has to a protector. He doesn't want to lose him."

"Well, his brother left him to deal with all of this alone anyway," says Julie.

"He probably didn't anticipate Jonathan confessing. We need to talk to the girl," says Brooks.

Julie closes her eyes and shakes her head. "This feels so wrong. These kids, they're so vulnerable. Jonathan's going to take the fall for something his brother did."

"Not if the victim talks," says Brooks.

"If he talks," says Julie.

"Let's wrap it up for now," says Brooks.

The officers return to the room where Jonathan sits. He somehow appears smaller, alone in the empty room.

"Am I going to jail?" he asks.

"Well, Jonathan, you have to understand this is considered a violent crime. That is serious. However, you are a minor, so that puts you under the Juvenile Delinquents Act. You don't have any previous charges but there will be some consequences. The truth is, there are still a lot of factors we have to consider, like how Daiji is doing. We would like to hear from him about all of this."

"What if he dies?" asks Jonathan.

Julie leans over and puts a hand on Jonathan's shoulder. "It's too soon to think about that, Jonathan. We are hoping he will be OK."

She straightens and looks at Brooks, who is cupping his chin, puzzled by the thirteen-year-old's bravado. He seems oblivious to the path ahead of him.

"I want to see him," says Jonathan. "I want to apologize."

Chelsey Health Centre

Anton Williams rushes to the nursing station of Four North, searching for Jason. He finds him assisting a patient with a puzzle in the common area. He catches his eye and hurries over.

"He's awake!"

"Really?" Jason says.

"Yes, just now. We were chatting in his room when he opened his eyes and made a joke."

"That's fabulous," says Jason.

He quickly rounds the corner with Anton on his heels. Jason looks around for the police officer who has been patiently waiting for a break in Daiji's condition.

"He went for a coffee," says Anton.

Jason and Anton step into the room to find an alert, smiling patient. The energy of the room is palpable and Daiji's face shines in the sunlight.

"Daiji, this is Jason. He is one of the people who have been caring for you," says Barbara.

Daiji smiles with his whole face and bows his head.

"It's a pleasure to meet you, Daiji. We are very happy that you are awake," says Jason.

Daiji smiles again.

"Can you hear me OK?"

This time, Daiji nods.

Sergeant Hannah appears in the doorway. "Is he awake?"

The elders smile with excitement. "He's awake," says Anton. "He understands what we are saying."

"Excuse me, everyone," says Jason. "I know you are eager to speak with Daiji, but it's imperative that we examine him further before we ask too many questions. The doctor will want to see him first."

Jason speaks directly to his patient. "Daiji, we need to examine you a little further, and then you can continue to visit with your friends, OK?"

Daiji nods.

"We understand," says Anton, ushering everyone out of the room.

Jason calls for the nurse on duty and they close the door. Sergeant Hannah finds a quiet lounge and calls Ramsey PD. One hour later, a doctor, nurse, and dietician leave Daiji's room. Jason stops to speak with the group.

"He's doing very well. We will have to take it slow. He has to practice eating and swallowing again, but he's doing exceptionally well. It's almost as if he wasn't in a coma at all."

"He's been taking time to heal," says Rudy.

Anton nods. "He's a very patient man."

"Indeed," says Jason.

"Can I question him now?" asks Sergeant Hannah.

"I believe so," says Jason. "He's expecting you."

Hannah goes into the room alone. Jason intervenes.

"Perhaps one of the elders could be present with him?"

"Yes, of course," says Hannah.

Barbara joins the police officer and closes the door.

"Daiji, I am Sergeant Michael Hannah. I'm part of the team investigating what happened to you. Your full name is Josef Brown—is that correct?"

Daiji speaks softly. "My given name is Josef Brown, but I am Daiji."

Yes, I understand that," says Hannah. "Daiji, you were staying on Nora Beach when you were attacked. Is that right?

"Yes, I was passing through Nora Beach. The surfers built me a teepee while I was there, so I stayed a little longer. I love the water."

"Do you remember what happened to you? How did you end up in the hospital?"

Daiji smiles. His face is calm, and he shows little sign of the brutal assault. "I am on a journey to teach the traditional ways to our people and your people."

"Yes, your family has told us about your journey. Are you reaching people?"

"Oh, yes. I am speaking to many about this."

"Did one of these people hurt you?" asks Hannah.

"This is not an easy journey," says Daiji. "There are many risks, but it's important to continue just the same." Daiji speaks slowly, cautiously considering every word. "The journey will hurt sometimes. I may hurt sometimes, but it is part of the healing. To heal, we first hurt."

As Hannah considers his next question, Barbara speaks.

"Daiji, we know you do important work. The police also have work to do. They need to make the beach safe for everyone. They want to know who hurt you. You must tell us who hurt you."

"I don't remember that," Daiji says with a smile. "I must rest now."

"OK, Daiji. We will let you rest. Perhaps we will speak again tomorrow. Thank you, sir," Hannah says.

Hannah leaves the room and calls Brooks.

Jimmy

The coastal rainforest is a lush, dense tapestry of green and gold. Lively cedars and graceful firs mingle with gnarled and decaying limbs and bush, breathing as an exotic mix of oneness. Jimmy Richards has been navigating this camouflage world for days, resting only to scavenge a few berries and take a light nap under a tree.

Finally, he's found it. The cabin looks as if it's being devoured by a thicket of moss and vine, and the small windows are plastered with leaves and mud. It has been hiding untouched, deep in the old growth, since his uncle Bernie left its threshold, unaware he would never return. A sudden heart attack while on a trip into town landed him in a morgue, and then he was cremated, compliments of the public guardian.

Jimmy heard of his uncle's fate weeks later when a relative sent word to child services requesting the Richards children be notified of their uncle's passing. There was no direct communication with the children; the vague assumption was that the message came from their mother.

This is the third time in his sixteen years that Jimmy has sought refuge at the shack. The first time is now but a vague memory as a child with his father, the second a desperate escape with his brother, and now an escape from himself.

The years of growth and decay test his navigational skills, but his uncle taught him to listen to the cues of the forest—a skill Jimmy learned to master. Once again, he has found his way by landmarks, terrain changes, and animal habitat. Bernie was low on supplies, but a few food tins remain and the rain barrel overflows.

Jimmy cups his hands, skims the top layer of leaves and dead insects, and takes a long drink. His bones ache and his feet are severely blistered. He steps inside, grateful for his uncle's old bunk, and drifts into a long sleep.

Ramsey Police Department

Julie and Brooks speak with Eugene while Jonathan waits with Constable Thomas in a room next door

"What happens next?" asks Eugene.

"Well, he confessed to a crime," says Brooks.

A shocked Eugene shakes his head. "What? Jonathan? That's so hard to believe! What's going to happen to him?"

"It's too early to say. He's thirteen and he has no previous record. A lot will depend on what happens to the victim. If Jonathan is charged with delinquency, then it's all up to the judge, and that's anyone's guess. It could be two years of industrial school, or worse if the victim doesn't make it. We are hoping it won't go that way. We are hoping Daiji will recover and talk, but so far he has not," says Brooks.

"The kid is thirteen. There are other ways to rehabilitate. If only we could keep it out of court," says Julie. "Of course, it doesn't help that the community is out for blood."

Eugene's face shows the stress of the unknown.

"Eugene do you think he is covering for his older brother?" asks Brooks.

Eugene can't hide his shock at being asked this question, not because he hasn't had his suspicions, but because he genuinely does not know how to respond.

"Is that what you think?" he asks.

"Something doesn't quite fit. This is a small, thirteen-year-old kid, without a mark or scratch on him. I don't know if he could cause so much damage to the victim. I mean, Daiji may have been hit by the logs of the structure, but Jonathan says he kicked and punched him."

"Jonathan said that?"

"Yes. Do you find that hard to believe?"

"Yes," says Eugene. "That is hard to believe."

"Has Jonathan been in fights before?"

"Not that I know of. Not in the couple years he's been with us."

"Any reports from school about bullying or not getting along with other kids?" Brooks asks.

"Again, no, not that I know of."

"What about Jimmy?"

"What about him?" asks Eugene.

"Is this something Jimmy could do?"

Eugene stares at both officers blankly. "I'm sorry, but I can't say. I mean, I'm not comfortable with this. I don't know what happened that night and I can swear to you that no one has confided in me. I really am as confused by all of this as you are. All I can tell you is that Jonathan, Jimmy, and Lisa are close, especially the boys. They've been through a lot together."

"What do you mean?" asks Brooks.

"Before they were sent to us, they were on the run. The two boys were taken from their family and forced to attend Alberni Residential School. I don't have to tell you about the history of that place. They did not do well there. Jonathan and Jimmy were abused. Jimmy, being older and tougher, took it a little better than Jonathan. Jonathan was not doing well—he was sick and traumatized, and they refused to let him see his brother.

"Jimmy disclosed to one of the workers that he thought Jonathan was going to die, so he got them out of there. The two of them were on the run for quite a while, hiding from school officials. They ended up staying with an uncle who was living on his own in the bush somewhere. They were off the grid for a time, but were later seen in town, and well . . . the kids weren't in school, you know how the story goes. Scrutiny, judgements, they were taken from their uncle and ended up with us."

"It sounds like Jonathan owes his brother a lot," says Julie.

"Do you know where the uncle lives?" asks Brooks.

"No idea," says Eugene. "He died a couple of years ago. He was in the bush somewhere on the coast."

"That's a big area," says Brooks. "OK, Eugene, there are still a lot of factors up in the air. Jonathan has not been formally charged yet. To let him go today, we need your guarantee that he won't disappear. This is an ongoing investigation. He will be released, but with conditions. It's important that no outings are planned in the next while and that Jonathan doesn't go anywhere. He should be picked up from school and supervised at all times. The school will have to be part of this. No play dates, no family visits, no after-school activities. Do you understand? We will have someone watching him as well."

"I understand. I will call a meeting at the home with his school contacts and his youth worker," Eugene says.

"Good. Constable Morneau, you will have to be part of those meetings."

"Yes, of course," says Julie.

"Will he be charged?" asks Eugene.

"We're trying to avoid that. He's a minor there are other measures we can take." Brooks is summoned to take a call. "Excuse me," he says to Eugene. "Constable Morneau will go over the particulars of the release with you."

He returns to his office. "Brooks here."

"Brooks, it's Hannah. I tried to reach you earlier, but they said you were interviewing one of the kids. Did you get anything?"

"We have a thirteen-year-old who says he did it, but we think he's covering for his brother. How are things there? Any news on our victim?"

"He's awake and he's talking."

"He's talking? He's OK?" says a bewildered Brooks.

"He's alive and well," says Hannah.

"That is good news!" says Brooks.

"Yes, but he seems to have a bit of a memory problem," says Hannah.

"Memory problem? That doesn't sound good. Does he remember anything at all?" asks Brooks.

"More like a selective memory problem," says Hannah.

"How selective?" asks Brooks.

"Well, he was doing fine until we asked about the who and why of the assault, and then he couldn't remember a thing. I don't know, maybe it's legit. It's hard to tell with these guys, you know. He's talking about his journey and taking risks, but nothing about the night in question."

"I see. Well, he hasn't been awake long. He may need some time."

"Yes, that's true," says Hannah. "The guy isn't even eating yet. We are fortunate to have gotten a word from him at all. He's a lucky guy, that's for sure."

"Are the elders with him?" asks Brooks.

"They haven't left his side. They were praying and chanting, and poof, he wakes up, just like that."

Brooks chuckles at Hannah's skepticism. "Poof, is it? Well, I guess we need more people like them."

"I guess so," says Hannah. "Maybe I should get some feathers."

Brooks laughs. "You need more than feathers for that prickly skin."

"Got that right."

"OK, Hannah, thank you for the call. Perhaps we'll have you hang tight for a day or two. See if his memory gets any better. Keep in touch."

"Will do," says Hannah.

Brooks steps back into the briefing room, where Julie is explaining the particulars to Eugene and Jonathan.

"I have some very good news," says Brooks, taking a seat next to Jonathan. "He's awake. Daiji's going to be OK."

"Oh, thank God," says Eugene.

Julie gives a quiet sigh of relief.

Jonathan quietly sobs and grabs a surprised Brooks for a hug—an unexpected reaction from the perpetrator.

"Can I see him now?" asks Jonathan.

Chelsey Health Centre

Sandra is at the fourth floor nursing station, filling out reports, when the phone rings. "Four North."

"Good morning. This is Sergeant Anthony Brooks from Ramsey PD. I have a special request regarding your patient Josef Brown, aka Daiji."

"Yes, Sergeant, I have been speaking to one of your officers who arrived yesterday. What's the special request?"

"We have a youth who says he is responsible for Daiji's injuries and wants to talk to him. He's thirteen years old, scared, and full of regret. We would like to grant him this request because we think he is covering for someone else. We're hoping we may get some truth from this meeting."

"I see," says Sandra. "Can't you speak with Daiji directly?"

"Yes, we've tried that, but he doesn't seem to recall the events. We are hoping this might jog his memory."

"Ah, yes. I can see how such a meeting could be beneficial to your investigation, but I'm not sure if it is in the patient's best interest. Daiji is the victim of a violent crime and has just found his way out of a coma. I don't know if it's a good idea right now to have a conversation with the person who assaulted him."

"I see your point, but you need to see this kid. He's not a big threat. I don't really think he's our guy, but he does know what happened. He is upset and remorseful and wants to apologize. It will help him in the long run, and may help us learn the truth."

"Well, Sergeant, I'll check in with our patient and see how he feels about it, then let you know."

Sandara arrives at Daiji's room and finds him resting comfortably. His shoulders are draped with a black cloth embroidered with a colourful thunderbird. On his table sits a carving of a wolf made by his father, who would tell Daiji stories about the secret wolf society, made up of heroes in life and death. The room has a slight scent of sage. He senses her presence, opens his eyes, and smiles.

"Hello," he says.

"Hello, Daiji. I'm so glad to see you awake. How are you doing?"

"I'm feeling very well, thank you." Daiji's voice is soft but clear.

"How's the eating going?"

"Good," he replies. "I was extra hungry. You have very good food here."

"You may be hungry," says Sandra, "but you need to take it easy. Not too much at first. It may take a little while to get back to your old self. You must have patience with yourself."

"Everyone is treating me well. I am very grateful to get myself back."

"So are we, Daiji," she says. "Daiji, I know the police have been asking you questions about the event that led to your injuries."

"Yes," he says.

"How do you feel talking about it? Were you OK with it, or was it painful?"

"It's fine to talk about it. I have been talking about it. It's part of the process. To heal, we must talk and learn more."

"I agree, Daiji. The police tell me the person, the boy who hurt you, has confessed."

"Oh," says Daiji.

"Yes. A thirteen-year-old says he was involved. In fact, this person wants to talk to you."

"Who is he?"

"His name is Jonathan Richards. I told the police I didn't think you were ready for this yet. You have just come out of a nineteen-day coma. You are learning to speak and eat and move all over again. We don't want you to relive any bad memories right now. This may not . . ." Sandra stops speaking. The weight of her words seems out of step with the sudden change of mood in the room.

Daiji has closed his eyes and is smiling a big smile. This small man who has been fighting for his life suddenly looks peaceful.

Sandra is speechless and moved by the unexpected reaction. "Daijj," she says. "Did you hear me?"

"Yes, yes," he says. "That is very good news. I will speak to Jonathan. Thank you, thank you for telling me. I am ready. He can come."

Ramsey to Chelsey

Brooks decides to make the trip with Jonathan himself. It's unusual and he will take a world of grief for doing it. He has a hunch that he needs to follow carefully, and if he's right, the true story will come out.

The circumstances don't show an intent to hurt. It's all too accidental. How can you charge a thirteen-year-old kid without knowing the whole truth? Before Jonathan is officially charged, Brooks needs to hear from the victim. He wants to see for himself how Daiji and Jonathan interact, and get a clearer view of what actually happened.

As the officer in charge, Brooks can advocate for special considerations under the juvenile court committee. If the boy shows remorse and apologizes to the victim, it will put him in a better position when facing the consequences. Besides, with all the speculation building in the community, Brooks will need every good deed he can muster.

Eugene accompanies them, as he has agreed to spend the night with Jonathan in Chelsey.

The four-hour trip is somber, as Jonathan seems to be lost in a nightmare of thoughts. "Did he say anything yet? What happens if he doesn't want to talk to me? Are you going to arrest me after we leave? Will I see him alone?"

"He has agreed to see you, Jonathan. Otherwise, this trip would not be taking place. I will drop you and Eugene off at the hotel to get lunch and pick you both up in a couple of hours. We will go to the hospital together."

Jonathan gives a nervous nod.

Ramsey Police Department

Julie has spent all morning putting out fires. The local press has caught a bloody scent on the Nora Beach assault and are clamoring for a lead.

"Bloodhounds!" Julie sputters and hangs up the phone. "How many times do I have to say nothing has been confirmed at this point and no charges have been laid? We are still investigating."

The town chatter has escalated based on conjecture, speculation, and bias. The mayor's office has come under attack for soft bylaws on transients and loitering. Tribal police are being roasted for not "controlling their people" and the youth home has been defaced. Protests downtown demand more attention to homelessness and poverty, and after the unintended reactions at the community meeting, the mayor isn't eager to wade in. Seems she can't see much personal gain in doing so.

On the other hand, her political rival, Christopher Stamer, has not. He sees an opportunity to highlight every grievance and issue he has been fighting for decades. Self-serving, perhaps, but whatever his motivation, Julie has agreed to see him, as he says he may have helpful information regarding the case.

Julie catches Hannah as he rushes by on his return to the office. She leaves her desk and catches him before he takes lunch.

"Sergeant Hannah, do you have a minute, please?"

"Just one, Morneau. I'm not punched in yet and I need lunch."

"I understand you're just back from Chelsey."

The detective looks annoyed. "Yes well, Brooks wants to follow a hunch. He didn't need me there."

"That's true I suppose," says Julie. "Did you see Daiji?"

"Yes, I saw him. He's doing well. I mean, that's what they're telling me, anyway. He has to start eating and moving again, but he managed to talk to me for a few minutes. He doesn't remember much. Or he's not saying much. I'm not sure what it is."

"He didn't say anything about the incident?"

"Nada, kind of brushed it off, like it wasn't important to him. Gave me nothing. Maybe he needs more time. I don't know. Maybe Brooks and the kid will get more of a reaction. We'll see. In the meantime, we need to charge this kid with something. Did you see the crowd outside City Hall? They're making a very big deal out of this, kid or no kid."

"I know," says Julie. "There are some tyrants out there. They don't care about evidence or circumstances. They just want blood."

"It's been like that since the beginning of time, Morneau. Where have you been? It's called justice. You know this guy. Don't you want someone to pay for putting him in a coma and leaving him for dead?"

"Yes, of course I do, but things are seldom black and white like that. We don't have all the information."

"The guy confessed, did he not?"

"Yes, but we think he's covering for his older brother."

"Based on what?"

"His brother went missing the day after the attack. He's the older sibling, the leader. There are no signs of force on the kid. Not a scratch. There are no prior incidents, either. He's a good kid, while the brother has a bit of a history."

"That's not enough and you know it. They were in on it together. Just bad blood. If you can't get them both, take the one who's wrapped in a big red bow. The Crown Counsel wants a delinquency charge," says Hannah.

"Crown Counsel is playing to the crowd and the media," says Julie.

"Maybe, maybe not. We have to do something right. The guy confessed! I have to go, Morneau. Let me know if you hear from Brooks."

"Will do, sir."

Chelsey Health Centre

Brooks, Eugene, and Jonathan take the elevator to the fourth floor. Jonathan looks defeated, flanked by the two men. Eugene can sense his distress and gives him a pat on the back.

"Jonathan, you're going to be OK." Eugene looks at Brooks for help. "Maybe this isn't a good idea. It's a lot of pressure."

The elevator dings as it arrives on the fourth floor. They step off and Eugene quickly pulls Jonathan aside.

"You don't have to do this, Jonathan. If this feels like too much, we can turn around and go back home right now."

Brooks glares at Eugene, attempting to process what's happening.

Jonathan hugs Eugene and begins to sob. "I don't know. I just don't know what to do."

Eugene clutches the young boy and looks at Brooks with panic and mistrust. "I don't know either, Sergeant. Shouldn't he have a lawyer present or something? We could be making a big mistake here. This is his future we're talking about."

Brooks senses panic. "OK, listen. I understand you're scared. Both of you. What you don't understand, Jonathan, is that this gesture will go a long way in your review." Brooks takes a step toward Jonathan. "You said you didn't mean for this to happen, and you want to apologize to Daiji, right? Make things better? Is that how you truly feel?"

Before Brooks can take another step, Jonathan breaks free from Eugene and bolts down the corridor to the stairwell.

"Jonathan!" shouts Brooks.

The thirteen-year-old dodges housekeeping and several wheelchairs and ducks into the stairwell. Brooks is slowed by the congested hallway, but quickens his pace after him.

"Oh my God!" shrieks Eugene. "He's gone!"

Jimmy

Jimmy's protesting stomach pulls him from his deep sleep and sends him on a search of his uncle's small rustic kitchen. He finds sardines, beans, soup, flour, salt, honey, oil, and a few utensils, including a well-used can opener. He helps himself to the beans and sardines, relieving the immediate pangs, and starts collecting wood in preparation for an afternoon fire. His heart warms with the fond memory of his uncle's cooking show, as he and Jonathan fondly referred to it. The first lesson taught them how a quick mix of flour, oil, salt, and powder will deliver a tasty bannock when roasted over an open fire. Jimmy's mouth waters thinking about it.

The few months he and Jonathan spent at camp, as his uncle called their stay with him, were happy times. Probably the best of his life. Once the horrors of Alberni faded into the background, Uncle Bernie taught his nephews about their ancestors and the skills of off-grid living. He told stories about their father Moe when he was a boy and how he liked to follow Bernie around. He also spoke about their mother, about whom the boys knew very little, as they were taken from her when Jonathan was still in diapers. They were raised in the early years by their paternal grandparents until they were taken from them, too, by the Indian agents.

Uncle Bernie told them about their maternal Cree heritage and how their mother, Irene, had a beautiful singing voice. She used to tell stories about searching for *mino-pimatisiwin*—the good life—and was sure she and his brother Moe would find it together along coastal British Columbia.

Bernie and Moe's family welcomed her here. She was excited about teaching her children to create the good life close to the earth, but sadly, she never achieved it herself. She, too, was a victim of residential schools, left with demons she could not escape. She never forgave herself for losing her children, and she left their father, never to be heard from again. Their father died from kidney failure, or as Bernie put it, he drank himself to death. Uncle Bernie decided it was his job to share what he knew with his nephews and was happy to have them in his life.

While living with their uncle, they learned to track, hunt, distinguish between edible and inedible plants, read the terrain, and protect themselves from hungry bears and stormy weather. All in a day's work, their uncle would say. Their profound attunement to nature and the earth was what Jimmy imagined home felt like—perhaps the closest connection he's had to a family.

He and Jonathan grew to love the forest. Jimmy was content to spend his time living among the giant firs and cedars, distinguishing between bird songs and sensing the approaching rain. These finely tuned skills became as natural as breath to him. He never wanted to leave and convinced himself that no amount of schooling would ever be as valuable as his forest lessons. His peace came to a screeching halt when a two-day excursion to town to secure supplies resulted in a scoop by family services. He and Jonathan were separated from the last of their family for good.

Jimmy never forgave the intrusion and grieved the jarring separation from his forest life for months to come. In the years that followed, the grief gradually subsided, only to be replaced by anger. An anger he managed to suppress for a time, but inevitably exploded when he least expected it. It forced him to leave his younger siblings and retreat into the embrace of the wild.

But his forest refuge, while comforting, can't begin to ease the torture in his mind. He has struggled with his decision to leave. How will his siblings survive the scrutiny and judgements alone? Now, he's no different from everyone else who left them.

When things get tough, Jimmy always runs, regardless of what he leaves in his wake. As far as he's concerned, his brother and sister are better off without him, free of the rage that threatened to smother and blind them as it did to him.

An Offer of Help

Julie sits at her desk, working through the last of the messages for the day. Damage control is draining. It's not accountability that irritates her; it's the lack of respect for individual rights and freedoms that upsets her the most. The uninformed deny the concept of innocent until proven guilty, personal circumstances and motivations, and factors beyond a person's control. Every crime has a complex story. Any cop with a conscience wants to get it right.

Her entire shift consisted of disputing rumors, handling media misinformation, listening to racist comments, and debunking conjecture and speculation. The world seems like a pretty ugly place right now. She admires Brooks for coordinating the unconventional meeting with Daiji to dig out the truth.

How can a thirteen-year-old who has no security or a trusted adult in his life deal with all of this? Why would Jonathan want to hurt Daiji? Why would he cover for someone else's senseless act? As her mind begins to take a disturbing journey down the rabbit hole, she's graciously pulled up by a voice at her desk.

"Working late, Constable Morneau?"

"Mr. Stamer. I wasn't expecting you to drop by. I did get your message. I'm sorry I couldn't get back to you. It's been a hell of a day."

"I figured as much, and it's Chris. Can I have a moment before you leave?"

"Yes, of course. We can go into Sergeant Brooks's office. There's more privacy there."

They walk the corridor to the corner office and take a seat. Julie glances at the family pictures lined up in the sergeant's bookcase.

"So, this is where the big dog plays?" says Stamer.

Julie smiles. "Yes, this is what twenty-five years will get you, I guess."

"Well, Constable, I understand you and Brooks have been working with one of the youths from Shannon House."

"We can't confirm anything yet, Chris. It's just not prudent. No official charges have been laid as of yet."

"Yes, I understand that. I want in on the case."

Julie looks at the well-respected lawyer, confused.

'What do you mean you want in on the case?"

"Let's just say I know what this kid is up against. This town wants a scapegoat and he's the perfect target: a vulnerable Indigenous child. He doesn't stand a chance, and this will go sideways really fast if the assistant district attorney wants to make an example out of this kid."

"I'm sorry, Mr. Stamer. Are you saying you want to represent this kid because children aren't afforded such luxuries in this jaded system we call the law? A delinquency charge will put him in the judge's hands."

"I am aware of that, Constable. What I am asking for is a behind-the-scenes role. There could be other options for this kid. We should try to keep him out of the court."

Julie smiles. "Just when I was sure the scum was winning. This is the best news I've heard all day."

"Good. I'm glad. So, fill me in. Where are we with this? Who has questioned him? I need to see him. Where is he?"

Chelsey Health Centre

Brooks sits at Sandra Braxton's desk. She generously donated the space for his use while she makes her last rounds of the day.

The sergeant is working the phones, recruiting help from Chelsey PD. Hospital security makes laps of the building inside and out. He knows how it looks. A senior officer transports a potential suspect, a youth in care, who then disappears? He cringes at the thought.

So far, everyone has agreed to keep things quiet. Eugene has contacted Shannon House under the illusion of checking in, but has received no alerts about Jonathan.

How could Brooks let this happen? Everything seemed to be under control. It was the guardian, not the youth, who pulled the alarm . . .

His intense thoughts are interrupted.

"Any luck, Sergeant Brooks?"

He spins around to see Sandra's friendly face. "I'm afraid not. This kid has managed to baffle me once again. Please call me Anthony." Brooks stands. "I'll give you back your office. Thank you so much. It was extremely helpful. I have to check in with security to see if they know anything."

"Poor kid, he must be terrified. He's trying to do the right thing, but probably doesn't know what that is at this point," says Sandra.

"Yes, I do understand that. What he doesn't realize is that this will only make things worse."

"If there's anything I can do," says Sandra, "please let me know."

"I appreciate that," says Brooks. "If you hear or see anything, please call Ramsey police. They can reach me."

"I will do that, Anthony," she says. "Good luck."

Hospital security has checked every stairwell, office supply room, and wing of the facility. They've patrolled the parking lot and looked inside every car. Jonathan may have escaped through the surrounding wooded area and made it to the highway. He could be hitchhiking in any direction.

Brooks drops by the hotel where Eugene is staying in hope of news. Eugene has nothing but regret. He blames himself for sounding the alarm.

"Perhaps I set him off. He was trying to hold it together and I was the release button."

"Don't blame yourself. I didn't see it coming, either," says Brooks.

He keeps the rest of his thoughts to himself. He knew it was a risk calling this kid's bluff. He was sure the interaction would somehow reveal the whole truth. What he didn't predict is how a thirteen-year-old with a history of abandonment, mistrust, and trauma might react to stress. The only thing this kid knows about life is that no one can be trusted. It makes sense that he ran.

Brooks places the blame where it belongs: squarely on his own shoulders. He's pretty damn sure the department will, too.

Eugene continues with his regret. "I should have known. He was becoming very anxious in the car, spewing out all those questions. 'What happens if he doesn't want to talk to me? Are you going to arrest me after we leave? Can I see him alone?' His mind was racing."

Brooks calls his office for messages. He has one from Julie. "Please call me when you get a chance. I have some good news for Jonathan. Chris Stamer wants to be involved behind the scenes and was asking questions about the investigation. I wasn't sure I should tell him where you were. Call when you have the time."

"Hmm, Stamer. He may be just the guy to fix this."

"Is there any news?" asks Eugene.

"No, just an update. What did you say he was asking us?"

"What do you mean?" asks Eugene.

"The questions, you said Jonathan was asking questions in the car. What were they?"

"Oh, he asked what happens if Daiji doesn't want to see him, and if you were going to arrest him, and whether he'd get to see Daiji alone."

"He wanted to see him alone? That's what he asked?"

"Yes, something like that."

"You mean he wanted to be alone with him?"

Eugene looks confused. "Maybe. Why? What are you thinking?"

"I think he wants to find out how this is going to roll. What's on Daiji's mind. What he remembers. Or maybe he wants to protect his brother," says Brooks. "Make his own deal!"

"Do you think he was just trying to ditch us?"

Brooks is pacing, connecting bits and pieces of the cases he's worked where perpetrators went on the run.

"The scared, the ones who know the evidence is stacked against them, take every measure to find proof themselves. Yes, maybe. Oh, this kid is keener than I gave him credit for."

Eugene looks at his watch. "Visiting hours will be over soon."

"Maybe," says Brooks. "But there are also less staff around. Maybe he's waiting for his chance. We need to get over there."

Brooks dials Julie and gets voicemail. "Morneau, I know it's late, but if Stamer is serious about helping this kid, he should probably get out here ASAP. Tell him to call me. I'm at the Regent Hotel."

Brooks and Eugene arrive at the hospital. Daylight is fading fast. The parking lot has emptied out, except for the night staff vehicles and a handful of lingering visitors. The perfect time for an unexpected visit.

Brooks takes the stairwell and sends Eugene to the elevator. They meet halfway down Four North, behind the security guard making his rounds. He stops and faces the two men.

"Hello, Marty," says Brooks. "Any sign of our young man?"

"I'm afraid not," says Marty. "Things have been pretty quiet. I'm about to head out to the parking lot for another pass."

"Great," says Brooks. "You know where I am."

"Yes, I do," he says.

Marty leaves the corridor and takes the elevator to the ground.

Brooks and Eugene arrive at Daiji's room and are met by the floor nurse.

"I know it's late," says Brooks. "Is it OK to have one quick word with him?"

"If it's OK with him," says Sheila, "it's fine with me."

"Thank you," says Eugene.

The private room is softly lit by a bedside lamp. Daiji is reading a small book.

"Hello, sir," says Brooks. "I'm sorry to bother you at such a late hour, but I was wondering if I could have a quick word?"

Daiji lowers his book and smiles. "Yes, OK," he says.

"I'm Sergeant Anthony Brooks from the Ramsey Police Department, and this is Eugene. We are traveling with a young man named Jonathan Richards. We were planning to come see you earlier, but it seems our young man got cold feet."

Daiji laughs. "Yes, I know this," he says. "He told me."

"Oh, he told you? Was he here?" asks Brooks.

"Yes, Jonathan was here." Daiji smiles.

Eugene breathes a sigh of relief. "Thank goodness. Where is he? Where did he go?"

"We had a good visit. I was happy to see him. He's a brave boy," says Daiji.

Brooks and Eugene stare curiously at Daiji.

"Can you share with me what you talked about?" Brooks tries his best to be patient.

"Jonathan is sorry for what happened to me. I told him I forgive him and that it wasn't his fault. Everything will be OK."

"You forgive him?" Eugene repeats.

"Yes," says Daiji. "He says he told you the story."

"Yes, sir, he did tell me a story," says Brooks. "But you see, I wasn't sure about the story. He has an older brother, Jimmy. Do you know Jimmy?"

Daiji smiles but says nothing.

Brooks continues. "I want you to know, Daiji, that I am trying to help Jonathan. He is a minor and I am trying very hard to keep him out of the system, but I need to know the truth of what happened. We thought he may be leaving out parts of the story. Parts that will help clear him."

Daiji smiles and nods quietly. "Detective, this boy Jonathan is not yet a man, but has lived the lives of ten men. He was not shown how to live in the world. He has no parents, no family, no love except his bond with his brother and sister. His parents could not care for him because they didn't know how. They, too, were hurt and neglected. The children are trying to take care of each other. They run, they hide. They are just trying to survive.

"Today, a thirteen-year-old boy came to me afraid and alone. He apologized for what happened. That was a big step for that boy. It heals me. It heals him."

"I understand," replies a humbled Brooks. "Will you be making a charge against him, then?"

"No charge," says Daiji. "But I would like to provide help for Jonathan."

"I'm glad to hear that," says Brooks. "Perhaps we can come up with some options for Jonathan together."

"Did he say where he was going?" asks Eugene.

"Yes, he was going back to the hotel. You just missed him."

Brooks and Eugene thank Daiji for his time. They make their way to the elevator and back to the parking lot.

"I hope that kid had the sense to go back to the hotel," says Eugene.

"He's there," says Brooks. "He doesn't need any pro-bono, hotshot lawyer. The kid just brokered his own deal. Not going to look good, though."

"What do you mean?" asks Eugene.

"The perpetrator of the assault pays a visit to the victim, alone?"

"But you haven't charged him, it's still an investigation, and he certainly didn't seem coerced! I won't tell if you don't," says Eugene.

Back at the Chelsey Inn, Eugene unlocks the room fifteen door and finds Jonathan sitting on the bed with his legs crossed, eating a bag of chips and watching TV.

"Well, well, look who's back!" says an animated Brooks.

"How did you get in?" asks Eugene.

"The man at the front desk let me in. I told him we got separated and he remembered me," says Jonathan. He straightens up and faces the two men.

"Yes, yes, separated. That's one way to put it I suppose," says Brooks, fighting to remain calm.

"I'm sorry, Mr. Brooks." Jonathan hangs his head.

Eugene sits next to Jonathan on the bed. "Jonathan, that was not smart. We were so worried about you."

"I'm sorry, Eugene. I got scared."

"I know you did, and that's partly my fault."

Brooks takes a deep breath. "So, Jonathan," he says, "you decided to see Daiji alone."

Jonathan looks a little surprised. "Yes, I did," he says.

"How did that go? I guess you forgot you're not supposed to see the victim of the crime alone, unsupervised. The crown wants to see someone pay for what happened to Daiji, and they could say you were going there to threaten him or force him to say what you want. There were no witnesses to this deal you made with the victim."

Eugene covers his mouth, his mind racing with the implications.

"There was a witness," says Jonathan. "We weren't alone."

"There was?" says Eugene.

"Who?" asks Brooks.

"Barbara. She's an elder. She was there the whole time. She bought me dinner."

Eugene hides a smile with his hand. Brooks stands and takes a deep breath, shaking his head.

"We will be heading back to Ramsey first thing tomorrow morning. Eugene, if this kid so much as goes to the toilet, you go with him."

"Gotcha," says Eugene.

"I'm not going anywhere," says Jonathan. "I promise."

Brooks forces a smile. "I will see you in the morning, Jonathan. If you don't want to be handcuffed to the bed, I suggest you do as Eugene says."

"I will," says Jonathan.

Brooks goes to his motel room and makes a call. "Listen, Stamer, we need to meet you at Ramsey PD tomorrow afternoon before our thirteen-year-old suspect guarantees himself a trial in adult court."

The Witness

Barbara, Rudy, and Anton are quietly discussing plans at Daiji's bedside.

"I have spoken with some of the council members who agree with your plan," says Rudy. "They will be happy to be involved with the boy's recovery. They are available to meet with us next week in Ramsey. We can join them at their band office to discuss options. If you aren't discharged in time, we can go without you and start the process. They have offered us a place to stay."

"I will be there," says Daiji.

Barbara stands and paces the room. She looks at Daiji, who senses her concern.

"Do you really think this is the best response for this boy?"

"Yes, Barbara," says Daiji. "I do. This is the purpose of our work. Blame weighs us down, buries our light. We must not focus on the violence. We must highlight forgiveness. It's the only way to heal trauma for both Jonathan and me."

"But doesn't he need to learn a lesson?"

"He learns by how we teach," says Daiji. "People heal when they are shown forgiveness. Jonathan does not know how to trust. He must experience compassion."

"What about consequences? What consequences does he experience for hurting an elder?" asks Barbara.

Daiji smiles. "Jonathan has been living the consequences of hurt and trauma his entire life. He was taken from his parents. They couldn't teach him because they hadn't healed themselves. He has faced one closed door after another. We have to stop this sequence of events. Forgiveness activates healing for everyone. I heal inside and outside because I forgive. I must show him the effects of forgiveness. We must change the way he experiences the world. We must be leaders, Barbara. This is my journey, my gift. Jonathan is my teacher, and I am his."

Barbara returns to her seat near her cousin. "You are an exceptional teacher, Daiji," she says.

Daiji smiles. "So is Jonathan."

Ramsey

Before heading back to the station, Brooks drops Jonathan and Eugene at Shannon House.

"Now remember, Jonathan, you have to meet with your lawyer Chris tomorrow. He's going to prepare you for the meeting with the elders and anything else that comes up. Daiji is not pressing charges, so we are trying to keep you out of the court. Chris is a decent guy, but more importantly, he is doing this for free. So don't go anywhere."

"I won't," says Jonathan. "I promise. I trust Daiji."

"OK," says Brooks, "that's good. I will see you tomorrow."

Jonathan and Eugene step out of the SUV and take a step forward when two men in a blue van drive up close to Jonathan, roll down the passenger window, and take a picture. Jonathan freezes, not sure what has happened. Brooks jumps out of the SUV and the van races off.

"What was that?" yells Eugene.

Brooks is giving orders into his radio. "Don't worry about it. It's the media. They think they have a story. Just go inside and don't talk to anyone about any of this. Jonathan, no phone calls, no questions from your teachers, nothing. If anyone has a problem with that, tell them to call me."

Jonathan nods and rushes inside.

Ramsey Police Department

Brooks heads down the hallway of Ramsey PD toward his office, tailed by an anxious Julie. He throws his coat and bag in the vacant chair in the corner.

"Sorry for stalking you, sir, but I need to update you," Julie says.

"That's fine, Morneau, it's been that kind of morning. What's going on?"

"Well, sir, the media are on to the fact that we have been questioning a youth from Shannon House. They even know his name."

"I'm aware," says Brooks, "and now they have a picture to put with the name."

"This kid needs protection," says Julie. "People are blowing this out of proportion and looking for a scapegoat. They think we have charged Jonathan."

"I have asked a car to do regular rounds at Shannon House for a couple of days until we can resolve this thing. I am meeting with Stamer in an hour to discuss extrajudicial measures involving the elders and members of the Nation."

"And Daiji?" asks Julie.

"It was his idea," says Brooks.

"Of course." Julie smiles. "I knew he would make all of this right. So, did he do it? Is Jonathan responsible for the broken ribs and head injury? Do we know what happened?"

Brooks stands up and closes the door to his office. "I don't know, Morneau. All I know is this man doesn't want to charge him. He won't say if the older brother was there, or even if he knows him. Jonathan is sticking to his story. He says he became upset and overreacted by pushing and kicking this guy. Daiji says the kid didn't mean to hurt him. It was an accident, a push, and the beams fell on him."

"That might account for the head injury, but there was direct bruising on his ribcage from being kicked," says Julie.

"That's what's difficult," says Brooks. "It sounds violent, but we have a teenager with no priors, a good kid by his guardian's accounts, and a victim who says nothing intentional happened. We just don't know if the older brother was involved or why he disappeared. Why would the kid take a chance on being charged with delinquency to protect a brother who has disappeared? That's a pretty grand gesture for a thirteen-year-old, don't you think?"

"I agree," says Julie.

"This kid is complex," says Brooks. "But Daiji seems to think he has been through enough, and that connecting him with the Nation and involving him in their healing traditions will be good for him."

"Can't argue that," says Julie.

"Oh, but someone surely will," says Brooks.

"Speaking of someone," says Julie, "Jenna Collins has been calling every couple of hours requesting a meeting. She, too, has heard the rumors and wants to know why she hasn't been informed."

"I bet she is," says Brooks. "Leave the crown prosecutor to me. The next time she calls, put her through."

Shannon House

Jonathan has dinner with Lisa in the dining room of Shannon House. The ten-year-old has missed her brother and can't speak fast enough to get him up to speed.

"The menu is changed now for the fall, so we won't have taco Tuesdays, but yesterday I had mac and cheese and that was good. My teacher is having a baby and that means we're going to have a new teacher for the rest of the year. Did you have a good trip, Jonathan?"

Jonathan slowly looks up from his plate of spaghetti, disregarding all her news. "Has anyone heard from Jimmy?"

"No. Jimmy is still gone, and he hasn't called anyone. I miss him. Where do you think he went?"

"I don't know," says Jonathan.

"Do you think he's dead?" asks Lisa.

"Jimmy's not dead!" Jonathan raises his voice, catching the attention of Stephanie, one of the workers. "Jimmy is too smart to be dead. He just needed to go away for awhile. He misses us too. I'm sure of it."

"Maybe we'll see him at Christmas," says Lisa.

Stephanie makes her way over to where Jonathan and Lisa are sitting. "How are you two doing?"

"We're fine," says Jonathan.

"We're glad you're back," she says.

"Am I allowed to go back to school?" Jonathan asks.

"It will be another week, Jonathan. I have explained the situation to your teachers, and they are collecting some work for you to look at over the weekend. I have volunteered to homeschool you until you get back. We hope it will soon be back to normal for you, Jonathan."

"Me too," he says.

Jonathan is tired, so he decides to skip the evening movie and head to his room. He takes out the notebook from his top drawer and starts to draw. He draws a teepee with strong logs and a white canvas. He draws a surfer like the one drawn on Daiji's canvas wall.

Then he draws a fire and flames. He remembers the sounds of the fire as it began to catch the canvas. He hears Lisa crying and yelling. Then he remembers pulling Lisa, running, and the sounds of the waves taking it all away. He turns the page of his notebook and writes the word *mino-pimatisiwin*. He closes the book and sinks deep under his covers.

"*Mino-pimatisiwin*, Jimmy."

He falls into a deep sleep, exhausted by a week of worry.

A few hours later, he's awakened by a piercing noise. What is it? He sits up in his bed, frozen with fear. Is he dreaming? It sounds like the fire alarm.

Shannon House is on fire!

"Fire! Everyone to the cafeteria. Stay calm!"

Stephanie and Eugene round up the children, making sure no one is missed. They line up in the cafeteria in their bare feet and pyjamas, facing the back exit like they have done many times before, but never in the middle of the night. There's a smell of smoke, and nervous, excited children frantically give their accounts of the frightening episode.

"I think the fire is close to my room."

"I can smell the smoke."

"I thought I was dreaming."

"Maybe we are at war," says a boy named Tommy, excited about the prospect.

The firefighters and police arrive on the scene and quickly contain the small fire outside the building. The wooden sign and banner that tells the story of Shannon Locket, for whom the house is named, was the target of a flaming cocktail. A cowardly tactic of intimidation. The police check the rest of the building and ask for everyone's accounts of the day, but suspect the perpetrators of the hateful act are long gone.

Jonathan is quiet and still a little numb. While he is no more responsible for this act of hate than anyone else, he feels as if he is. A feeling he has carried with him for a long time. He felt it at Alberni when they cut his hair and forbade him from seeing his brother. He lived it when they took him from his only known relative, Uncle Bernie, and he feels it now. He doesn't know when it started or why it's there. He just knows it doesn't matter if you are good or bad. Just when you think things are OK, they suddenly aren't. Just when you believe in someone, they're gone, and people will always think it's your fault.

The all-clear is given and the children make their way back to their rooms. Jonathan spends the rest of the night with his eyes open.

Ramsey Police Department

On Monday morning, Julie, Jonathan, and Eugene arrive together. Jonathan is under attack by persons unknown and requires a police escort. They settle into chairs in the conference room, waiting for Christopher Stamer and Brooks to arrive.

Jonathan lowers his eyes to the floor and grips the armrests of his chair. He is prepared to accept his fate. He's tired. There's nothing left to do but take it. He will be punished for ever setting foot on Nora Beach.

He speaks quietly to Julie. "My picture is in the paper. They know the police have been asking me questions and they think I am a criminal."

"I know," says Julie. "Remember, you haven't been charged with a crime. People like to make up stories and find someone to blame. The truth will come out eventually and they won't be able to blame you anymore. You will get through this, Jonathan."

"Where is Daiji? Is he here? He said he was coming to Ramsey."

"He will be here. He is meeting with the elders and they are deciding how best to help you."

Julie's attempt at comfort is interrupted by the arrival of Brooks and Christopher Stamer. Brooks smiles at Jonathan.

"How are you today?" he asks.

Jonathan tries to smile. It's hard not to respond to the charismatic Brooks.

"Jonathan, I would like you to meet your lawyer, Christopher Stamer," Brooks says.

Stamer has an allure of his own. He stands over six feet tall and wears a smile that lights up the room. His blond hair is longer than one would expect from a frequenter of the court and a direct contrast to his blue suit and matching tie, which sit under a significant red beard.

Stamer walks over to Jonathan, who stands and shakes his hand. "It's a pleasure to meet you, Mr. Richards. Are you ready to play ball with me?"

Jonathan stares at the vibrant Stamer, not knowing whether to smile, nod, or ask for an explanation.

"We're going to get through this, Jonathan. All of us together. I am going to see to it," Stamer says.

"Thank you," Jonathan replies.

Stamer takes his place at the table.

"So, Jonathan, I know things have been tense for you these last few days, with the fire last night and the media the day before. How are you doing?" asks Brooks.

"I'm OK. I mean, it's a bit scary. I think I should just do whatever I need to do so people will leave us alone. I don't want anyone else to get hurt."

"That's what we want too, Jonathan." Stamer throws a quick glance at Brooks. "Sergeant Brooks and Constable Morneau have been working hard to gather as much information as possible to keep you from being charged. But because you voluntarily gave a statement that you hurt this man, Daiji, you have admitted to a crime. It is my understanding that Daiji has not disputed anything you have said. Is that your understanding, Jonathan?"

An officer enters the room and bends to speak into Brooks's ear. Brooks looks annoyed.

"Excuse me, everyone, I must attend to this," he says. "Jonathan, Chris will fill you in on next steps." He gives him a wink and leaves the room.

Brooks makes his way to his office, where an insistent visitor waits: crown prosecutor Jenna Collins.

"Hello, Jenna. So glad to see you," he says. "I've been meaning to call."

"What's happening, Brooks? Why haven't you been communicating with Crown Counsel on the Richards case?"

"Because it's not a case, Jenna. The youth hasn't been charged. I was preparing to fill you in on our plan to get the First Nations Youth Justice Committee involved."

"The kid gave a statement, and you didn't charge him?"

"That's right. We needed more evidence. I needed to talk to the victim. The kid gave a statement, but the victim, Daiji, doesn't want to press charges. The two have met and Jonathan apologized. Daiji wants to bring him into the First Nations community to participate in their cultural programs. He is going to take him on and mentor him. Their Youth Justice Committee have agreed to meet with us."

"Well, you have this all tied up in a neat, pretty bow, don't you, Anthony?"

"That's my job, Jenna. To solve crimes and find the best possible outcome. I know your cold heart loves the tough-on-crime approach, but this is a thirteen-year-old boy with no priors."

"This is a violent—very violent—crime, Sergeant, that your suspect apparently admitted to. We should have been informed. This needs to go before a judge."

"We needed more information. It wasn't cut and dry. We had reason to believe he was covering for someone."

"What someone? There's another suspect?"

"No, there's no other suspect."

"You're losing me, Brooks."

"The victim of this crime says there was no one else, but until we heard from him, we weren't sure."

"What about the girl? The suspect's statement says his sister was with him."

"Yes, the ten-year-old was there."

"Did you question her?"

"No, I didn't question a ten-year-old, because the thirteen-year-old said she had nothing to do with it and the victim says there was no crime."

"What are you hiding here, Brooks?"

"I'm not hiding anything, Jenna, unlike you, who seems to be burying any semblance of morality."

"Conscience has no place in the law, Sergeant."

"Clearly not, Jenna. Listen, it's clear cut. The victim does not want to press charges and the kid has no priors."

"I might like to hear from the witness," says Jenna.

"Lisa? You want to traumatize a ten-year-old when you have testimony from the accused and the victim?"

"Maybe we need more."

"Maybe you need more, Jenna. You need more security in your position, maybe? You need to present the mayor with a solution to the right-wing pushback she's getting over policies she hasn't had the motivation to advance on her own?"

"I'm not sure extrajudicial measures are enough here, Brooks. What kind of message does it send? He's vulnerable, I understand that. He's also a misguided youth who has no parental oversight, and now that job falls to the state. You know this!"

"I don't think you do understand, Jenna. We are policing and criminalizing our most marginalized populations. Why do you think these schools and detention centres are closing down? They don't work! We have to respond to trauma and poverty with culturally appropriate support, not industrial schools!" Brooks lowers his volume. "You know what those places are like."

Jenna continues to state her case. "He's at high risk for criminal activity. These youths should be policed more, not less! These kids can't just kick seniors around on Nora Beach and get away with it."

"I'll tell you what, Jenna. You meet with the victim, the accused, and our lawyer tomorrow for a discussion about the proposed measures for the kid, and then decide if you think it's enough."

"Our lawyer? Juvenile cases don't have lawyers. Are you familiar with the Juvenile Delinquents Act, Brooks?"

"A Good Samaritan offered himself up to make sure this plays out right."

"What are you talking about, Brooks?

"Chris Stamer has agreed to lend his advice on this one."

Jenna Collins looks as if she's watching an oncoming train. She glares at the cocky sergeant, collects her belongings, and heads for the door.

"Let my office know the time of this special meeting, Brooks."

"Will do," he says.

Outside Brooks's door, Stamer is almost run over by the crown prosecutor, who seems to be in quite a hurry to leave the Ramsey PD.

"I'm just on my way out," Stamer says to Brooks. "We're done for now. The kid should be fine. He understands he has to accept any suggestions the band has for him. What did Collins want?"

"Oh, you saw her?"

"Barely. She blew by like the hurricane she is. She didn't look happy."

"She wasn't thrilled to hear you were involved," says Brooks.

"I'll take that as a compliment," says Stamer.

"Well, it's the only one you'll get from Jenna. She's actually considering questioning the sister."

"The sister? How much does she know?"

"Everything, I guess. She was there." Brooks sighs, anticipating a complication.

"No one with any ounce of integrity would bring her into it," says Stamer. "We have the victim, who doesn't contest anything."

"Yes, well, Jenna Collins lacks that quality, so she may insist," says Brooks.

"I can't see it, Anthony. You have everything you need here. A thirteen-year-old boy with no priors—a First Nations boy with a history of trauma. I mean, if we have to play that card, we will. His reaction to Daiji was not intentional. It was defensive. Frankly, I don't think we'll need to go there. This kid needs a mentor. He needs to learn about traditional recovery and wellness, which the band seems to be offering. Don't worry about Jenna Collins."

"I hope you're right, Chris."

A Good Day

Jonathan and Eugene arrive an hour early at Conference Room A at Ramsey Courthouse. Jonathan hasn't slept and feels unprepared to hear how a community of adults will decide his fate. Despite reassurances from Brooks, a confident speech from his lawyer, and hopeful predictions from Eugene, only one thing rings in his head: don't buy into any of it.

Life doesn't always go the way you think, hope, or pray it will. You can be born to parents you never see and find a friend who stops being friendly. The good teacher suddenly gives up and your only brother runs away. Life is anything but predictable, that's for sure. What will happen today is anyone's guess, and Jonathan is prepared to take whatever comes. It doesn't feel good, but it doesn't feel bad, either. Just a familiar numb feeling.

Brooks and Stamer are going over notes at the end of the table. Four elders from Nuu-chah-nulth First Nations arrive and take their places around the table. Jonathan recognizes Barbara, who smiles and nods at him. Brooks introduces Stamer to them, and they all shake hands.

Jenna arrives and takes her place opposite the elders. She, too, is introduced by Brooks and receives polite nods from all. She looks blankly at Jonathan and then turns away to shuffle papers in her briefcase. Jonathan recognizes that look, and while he cannot articulate the judgmental air of racism it carries, he knows what it means and, more importantly, how it feels. She assumes his guilt, his proneness to misstep, and tendency to make bad choices. In her eyes, he's guilty by birth.

Jonathan feels his breath becoming unsteady, shallow. His stomach churns and his palms are beginning to sweat.

Daiji is not here. He probably changed his mind. Perhaps the elders talked him out of cooperating with a troubled orphan and they all want to teach me a lesson. Maybe they are right. I deserve to be punished, for entering a man's place uninvited and leaving him there to die. It doesn't matter now. I must do this for Jimmy. Nobody else knows him like I do. He's a good brother.

Jonathan's thoughts are interrupted as the conference room door opens and Julie and Daiji enter.

"I'm sorry we're late."

Barbara stands and embraces Daiji. They exchange words in their native language and smile. Julie leads Daiji to the end of the table, near Stamer, but he stops, scans the room for Jonathan, and sits next to him instead. He looks deeply into the young boy's eyes, gently touches his shoulders, and whispers in his language, an exchange Jonathan returns. Jonathan releases a smile from his tense face and takes a pause from his spiraling thoughts.

The room has gone silent. Brooks, Stamer, Eugene, Julie, the elders, and even Jenna are captivated by the exchange, and share a moment of pause. An extraordinary act of compassion has the power to touch everyone who witnesses it. An experience not often felt in a courthouse. An act that changes lives.

Brooks breaks the silence. "Jenna, I would like you to meet Daiji. He has recovered from the incident on Nora Beach, and as you can see, is motivated to work with Jonathan on a mentoring program with the kind support of the Nuu-chah-nulth elders.

Daiji, Jenna is the crown prosecutor and wanted to sit in on this meeting to ensure you were being treated fairly, so to speak."

"It's a pleasure," says Jenna. "Can I get your full name for the record, please?"

"Yes, of course," says Daiji. "I was born Josef Brown from the Tseshaht Nation. My parents were Sadie and Malcolm Brown."

"Thank you, Daiji."

"OK," says Brooks, "let's get started. In my investigation, I have learned that Jonathan Richards, as he has voluntarily admitted, was in a confrontation with Josef Brown, known as Daiji, on July 27. Jonathan heard Daiji was a shaman who lived on the beach, and he and his sister Lisa wanted to visit him.

"Jonathan was speaking with Daiji when a disagreement broke out. Jonathan was upset and pushed Daiji, who was standing in the teepee and showing him some carvings. Daiji resisted the push and put his hands on Jonathan's shoulders. Jonathan then kicked and punched Daiji. This time, Daiji fell against the wall. The accused continued to kick Daiji in the upper body. One of the logs supporting the teepee came loose and fell on his head, knocking him unconscious. Jonathan and Lisa left and Daiji was found outside. It is unclear to both the accused and Daiji how he got outside the teepee."

The words are piercing. Jonathan lowers his head in deep regret while listening to the account.

"Jonathan, was this your statement?" says Jenna.

Jonathan nods.

"I'm sorry, Jonathan, you have to speak your answers out loud."

"Yes," he says.

"Daiji, is this how you remember the incident?"

"I agree with Jonathan's account, but I would like to add something to it, if I may."

"Yes, of course," says Brooks.

Jenna and Stamer lean in to listen to this addition.

"I would like to acknowledge that I am partly to blame for Jonathan's actions. I was asking questions about the Richards family. I am a stranger to Jonathan, and I had no right to do this. This young man has had a difficult childhood. He has a traumatic history that includes abuse in a residential school. He lost his family because they were unable to care for him. They, too, were victims of crimes. This was not Jonathan's fault. Jonathan's actions can be understood when considered in this context. This is how we react to trauma. I know this. I should have been more delicate with Jonathan. He is a good person."

Stamer sits back and smiles. "We agree, Daiji. Jonathan reacted to past trauma and did not really mean to hurt you. If you understand this and forgive him, then it's our hope that Jonathan's rehabilitation could proceed with measures more suitable to the Nuu-chah-nulth's traditions. Wouldn't you agree, Jenna?"

Jenna looks around and realizes the consensus of the room is for extrajudicial measures to proceed. It would not be prudent to disagree.

"It was a violent crime," she says, pausing to look directly at Jonathan, who lowers his eyes to the floor. "In most cases like this, I would push for more court involvement. However . . ." Jenna pauses again, as if she can't believe her own words. "In this case, it doesn't seem prudent to do so, considering the victim's—ah, Daiji's—perspective. I would be interested in hearing what the Nation has in mind for Jonathan's rehabilitation."

The chief administrator of the Youth Justice Committee for Nuu-chah-nulth responds.

"We are prepared to do that. We understand that both the accused, Jonathan Richards, and the victim, Daiji, agree the assault was unintentional, and that Jonathan has admitted he made a mistake and regrets what happened. Daiji has shown us by example that acceptance and forgiveness are the key steps in healing. Because of this, we are willing to take Jonathan into our Nation and work with him in the Circles of Support Program. Jonathan will live in our community with one of our sponsor families of his origin. He will participate in healing ceremonies and learn the traditional language and practices of our people for at least one year, and for as long as he wishes to continue there after.

"He will do volunteer work in the community with a group we decide is satisfactory to his rehabilitation for a period of one year.

He will be helpful to his sponsor family and participate in family and community activities.

"We believe in family strength and want our children to reclaim and be proud of their heritage. We also know that children teach each other. We would like for Jonathan's sister Lisa to also become part of our community, and live with and learn from her brother.

"Jonathan will meet with his mentor every week to learn the spiritual lessons of his ancestors and be guided in his healing journey. In this case, Daiji has agreed to be his mentor."

Barbara speaks: "We feel this will be especially beneficial for Jonathan, as he will learn first-hand the power of forgiveness and compassion to change lives. We hope this will inspire him to develop his gifts and become a mentor himself.

"I would like to say this is an exceptional program designed for Jonathan by the extraordinary kindness of the man who was injured in this crime. Therefore, it will be an important and valuable learning opportunity for this boy. If we are all in agreement, we would ask Jonathan to join us tomorrow at the band office to discuss the details and plan his move."

Stamer sits straight up. "Exceptional! I don't remember ever hearing of such a fitting and progressive approach to youth justice. I have no doubt this approach will help steer Jonathan's future in a positive direction. Wouldn't you agree, Jenna?"

Jenna Collins is unusually speechless. She sits silently, lost in what she has just witnessed. Brooks casts a glance at Stamer, who cannot resist the moment.

"Jenna?"

"Yes," she says. She seems startled by the question.

"Are you in agreement with the conditions the elders have put together? It's groundbreaking, isn't it?" he says.

Jenna rouses from her daze. "Yes. Yes, of course. I must agree with my colleague Mr. Stamer. This is an exceptional, albeit unusual, response to youth crime. It is indeed quite inspiring. I would like to thank the Nuu-chah-nulth nations for coming together today and displaying their commitment to this program. Of course, we will need some signed copies of your proposal, but I am satisfied that justice has been done in this case."

Brooks explodes into a smile. "Well, on that note, Jonathan, it looks like you have a plan in place and there will be no need to take it any further. Are you agreeable to meet tomorrow to discuss the details of your plan with the nation?"

Jonathan looks a little stunned. He cautiously smiles. "Yes, I will, if Eugene can get me there."

Eugene laughs. "I'll get you there, Jonathan, don't worry about that. And Lisa, too, if appropriate."

"Yes, that would be a good idea," says Barbara.

"OK, then we are set to go," says Brooks. "Thank you all for attending."

Jonathan follows Eugene and the others through a back door and into the manicured courtyard. The afternoon sun feels warm. There's a smell of freshly cut grass, and a small sparrow splashes in a birdbath, misting its tiny feathers. Jenna Collins rushes to her car on her way to her next case. The elders stop and chat, lingering in the warm air.

Jonathan closes his eyes and lifts his face to the sun. Brooks pats him on the back and Eugene congratulates him. The voices around him are like quiet murmurings in the background. He feels light, unburdened, like it's the last day of school. How he wishes he could always feel this way.

Stamer hands Brooks a file.

"What's this?" asks Brooks.

"Have a look," says Stamer.

Brooks scans the document. It's a police report from two years ago for a fourteen-year-old Jimmy Richards, who was accused of an assault against a thirteen-year-old on school grounds. The report was sealed, as the youth was underage, and therefore could not be used in any subsequent case. Brooks reads the statement of the accused.

"'I don't know why it happened. Sometimes I get a brain fog and I have to fight my way out. It's like my brain gets fuzzy and I don't know what I'm doing.'" Brooks looks up at Stamer. "Almost word for word."

"Looks like your hunch is right. Jonathan was likely covering for his brother and used what he heard in the past. He probably thinks this is what happened to his brother again. In his mind, Jonathan sees his brother as innocent, not knowing what he's doing."

"He may be right," says Brooks. "What are you doing with this?"

"I did some snooping, just in case we needed it."

"It was sealed," replies Brooks.

"I understand that, but I thought if Jonathan knew we had it and we were on to his cover up, he might loosen his story. It was just an insurance policy in case things went differently. This kid doesn't deserve to go down for this. Thankfully, we didn't need it. It looks like he will benefit from his own brave act. That's real justice."

"Yes, it certainly is," says Brooks. "Remind me to look you up if I get myself into a tangle."

Stamer laughs. "Anytime, Anthony."

A buoyant Eugene extends his hand to Brooks and Stamer. "I can't thank you enough for helping Jonathan," he says. "He looks like he's in a bubble right now."

The three men look at a distracted Jonathan.

"I'm glad it worked out," says Brooks.

"You can thank Daiji for that. He really stepped up when we needed him," says Julie.

"The kid deserves a break," says Brooks. "I still think he was covering something up, but regardless, he will benefit from the Nuu-chah-nulth program."

Jonathan is oblivious to the banter. He looks around the courtyard, with its cobblestones and pruned hedges. He notices a butterfly fluttering past, as if it too has slowed down to smile at the day. The sky is an exquisite blue, and the wind softly whispers in his ear. He smells the fragrance of the nearby trees. The elders' faces shine as they smile and laugh with each other.

Jonathan stops and soaks it in—this feeling that he never wants to let go of. He looks to the horizon, beyond the entrance of the courthouse. Across the street, on a small bluff overlooking the city park, a familiar figure stands near a tree. Jonathan stares, and tries to extend his gaze, as if he could travel there through space.

It's his brother. It's Jimmy. He came back!

Jonathan's attention is broken by Eugene, who is guiding him toward the car. Jonathan stops. "Wait."

"What is it?" asks Eugene.

Jonathan looks back at the tree, scanning the area, but he can't see Jimmy anymore.

"What is it, Jonathan?" Eugene asks again.

Jonathan pauses and shakes his head. "Nothing. I thought I saw something. Please, Eugene, can I go to the park for a few minutes? Just a few minutes."

"Go ahead. I'll be right behind you."

Jonathan doesn't respond, but races across the street without waiting for the crossing light.

"Geez, Jonathan, be careful!" Eugene calls out. "This kid is going to be the end of me."

"Sounds like he's not the only one who needs a break from it all," says Julie.

"Once we get the program in place for him and Lisa, things should settle down. I hope the press will lay off," says Eugene.

"They will," says Julie. "We're giving a statement later today to satisfy the hounds."

"That helps," says Eugene.

Jonathan climbs the small hill behind the park. He reaches the tree where he saw Jimmy, but only finds a crow looking at him suspiciously.

I know I saw him.

He scans the field, the benches, the forest, and across the road.

He can see Eugene making his way over, but no Jimmy. Jonathan quietly walks toward the forest and softly calls his name.

"Jimmy! Jimmy! It's me, Jonathan."

The only response is the rustling leaves. Jonathan sits against a large oak on the edge of the forest and begins to cry.

Now I'm losing my mind, too. I miss you, Jimmy. I want you to know it's OK now. I fixed it. You would be proud of me, Jimmy. You can come back to us.

He looks around again. A dog is chasing a ball a few hundred metres away as his owner runs behind. Children line up for the slide in the park. But there's no sign of Jimmy.

He quickly wipes away his tears as he hears Eugene approach.

"Jonathan, what are you doing up here?"

"Nothing. I just need to be alone."

"I understand. You haven't had much of that lately. I know change is scary, Jonathan, but I think this move will be really good for you and Lisa."

"I know," says Jonathan.

"You know, sometimes good things come out of bad things, like it was meant to happen this way. Maybe some good things are in store for you and Lisa."

Jonathan nods. "I just wish Jimmy was with us, that's all."

Eugene senses Jonathan's struggle and sits next to him under the giant oak.

"Jonathan, can I share something with you?"

"Yes," he says.

"I admire you."

Jonathan looks at Eugene, surprised by his words.

"I admire your strength. You have experienced so much loss for a young man, and yet you've been so brave these last few weeks. Of course you miss Jimmy. I'm sorry he's not here with us. It must be a worry for you."

Jonathan nods again.

"Jimmy is smart. He's managed to get through some pretty rough times. You both have. He has taught you well. I'm proud of you for apologizing to Daiji. That's brave. You are braver than a lot of adults I know," Eugene says.

"Jimmy is brave and smart," says Jonathan. "He saved my life. I was ready to give up at Alberni. They were trying to change who I was. Jimmy said they were trying to wash our culture out of me, make me like them. They did horrible things to us, but Jimmy saved me, got me out. We spent many nights outside before we found Uncle Bernie, but Jimmy had food for us and lit fires to keep us warm. I wouldn't have made it without Jimmy."

"You have a very strong bond with Jimmy, Jonathan. That will never change. You will hear from him again. I'm sure you mean as much to him as he does to you. I think he has proven that already, and so have you."

Jonathan looks at Eugene and forces a smile.

"OK, let's go Jonathan," Eugene says. "I think you deserve a celebratory lunch. What do you say? The Green Shed for lunch?"

Jonathan's eyes open wide. "Yeah!"

They leave the giant oak and walk down to the playground, past the kids and the dog. Jonathan takes a few glances over his shoulder and decides his vision was just wishful thinking. They're crossing the street and heading for Eugene's car when they hear a voice from the courthouse steps.

"Eugene, Jonathan, hold up." It's Stamer. "I want to tell you something. I have been speaking with the council—ah, the elders—and they have agreed that you can volunteer with my firm once a week."

"Your firm? What will he do there?" asks Eugene.

"Well, more like my headquarters. I am planning to run in the federal election next year. We will be discussing my platform—I mean, the policies I will be pushing in the next year or so. These are important policies, some of them related to youth justice reform. I think it will be a good place for Jonathan. Jonathan, your case is a good example of the way the law should work for kids. We are also pushing for more housing and laws around foster care. I think you may benefit from this experience, Jonathan. After all, you kids will have to fix this messed-up planet someday. What do you think? Are you up for it?"

"Will I still get to see Daiji?"

"Yes, of course. Daiji will be your mentor and cultural counselor. This will be for your volunteer requirement."

"That sounds great," says Eugene.

"Yes," says Jonathan. "I would like that."

"Great, great," says Stamer. He pats Jonathan on the back. "We are going to do great things, kid, you and me."

Jonathan smiles a big smile. It's a good day.

A Family

Lisa is unusually quiet on the drive. Goodbyes are exchanged at the Nuu-chah-nulth band office, and Anton agrees to drive Lisa and Jonathan to meet their new foster family. Jonah and Mary Marcel and their three children live in the First Nation community of Conuma. The village of fifteen hundred residents sits in the snug Conuma valley below the prominent rocky summit for which it is named. Elders revere the mountain as a spiritual place, a place to find clarity and guidance. Mary and Jonah Marcel were born and raised here. They built a home on the sacred ground passed down from generations of families before them.

Lisa wonders how they feel about having another ten-year-old girl. They already have three children: Duncan, Samuel, and Lilly. Lilly will be Lisa's new sister. Lisa has never had a sister. What if Lilly looks funny, talks funny, or doesn't like Lisa? What if she thinks Lisa looks funny or talks funny? Lisa pushes her forehead into the window on the passenger side of the backseat and tries to focus on the waves that move as quickly as her thoughts.

It's a scenic route that meanders alongside Rosie Bay, just like Eugene said it would. It's not that far from Ramsey. They can go into town to shop, and if they have time, they can visit Eugene and some of their friends. "Visit anytime," he said. Jonathan will see the medicine man every week and some days Lisa can go with him. She liked his carvings.

She was so happy when Jonathan burst into her room to tell her he won't be sent away, that they can stay together and live with a good family. She was happy about her new brothers and sister, but now her stomach feels sick. She'll have to go to a new school, meet new teachers, make new friends, and show everyone how smart she is. And what about Jimmy? Three are stronger than two. How can they be strong without Jimmy? She breaks free of her mind and looks at Jonathan, who is staring out the other window.

"Jonathan, what if Jimmy comes back and he can't find us?" she asks.

Jonathan takes her question like a punch in the stomach. "I don't know. Someone will tell him. He'll find us. Jimmy will find us if he wants to."

Jonathan senses her anxiety. She is nervous, too, like they're about to step on shifting ground.

"It's OK, Lisa," he says. "Eugene and Daiji say this is a good place."

Lisa gives a reluctant nod, turns back to the window, and continues to bite her nails.

"OK, you two, we're here," says Anton.

They turn down Northwood Street, pull into a gravel driveway, and park in front of a brown wooden house with a red door. A covered deck looks out on a fenced front yard with cedar and maple trees. The leaves have turned red and gold. Smoke swirls from the chimney.

Mary and Jonah Marcel step onto the deck and wave to Anton. He is the first out of the car.

"Good afternoon Jonah, Mary," he says. "It's nice to see you again."

"Nice to see you! How was the drive?"

Jonathan looks at Lisa. "Let's go."

Jonathan and Lisa slowly step out of the car and walk up to the porch. The Marcel children have also come out to meet them. Anton makes the introductions and Mary invites them inside.

The oldest boy is tall, with short black hair and brown eyes. He is quiet and has a friendly face. He takes Lisa's bag for her and gives her a quick smile.

"We are happy to have you here with us," says Mary. "Duncan will bring your bag to your room." She touches the head of a little girl who is holding her hand. "This is Lilly. You two will share a room."

Lilly shyly smiles at Lisa, not letting go of her mother's hand. They are almost the same size, with Lilly being slightly taller. Her long braid is tied with a yellow ribbon that matches her yellow T-shirt.

"Do you want to see our room?" she asks.

Lisa smiles, surprised that she owns half of a room. "OK," she says.

She follows Lilly to the end of the hallway and into a large room. It is painted a pale yellow, and there are two beds and pink curtains. Lilly has a bright pink and white mandala hanging on the ceiling above her bed. Each of the corners is pinned, creating a canopy. Lisa admires the effect.

"We can put one over your bed, too, but my mom wants you to pick the one you like best."

"OK," says Lisa.

Jonathan is shown to a room upstairs, which he will share with Samuel. Samuel is twelve and has straight brown hair that almost reaches his shoulders. His eyes are green like Jonah's. He talks non-stop to Jonathan while showing him the room and his collection of records and comics.

"You can read them if you like, and play the records, as long as you take care of them. The record player is over there." He points to a brown case in the corner. "Do you have any?" He glances at the bag in Jonathan's hand.

"No," says Jonathan.

"You can put your bag there. That's your closet," says Samuel.

Next, Samuel takes him downstairs to Duncan's room.

"Duncan has his own room," he says. "Because he's the oldest, as if that's important. But it protects us from his terrible guitar-playing."

Mary then takes Jonathan and Lisa on a tour of the house, pointing out the bathrooms—one upstairs and one downstairs—and the garden out back where they grow vegetables. A large cat stretches on the railing, as if being disturbed from his nap. Jonathan rubs his fur, and he pushes his head into Jonathan's hand.

"That's Eddie," says Mary.

Jonathan smirks.

"Yes, I agree. It's a strange name for a cat, but Duncan thought it was a good idea," she says. "There's a trail out back leading into the forest, where you can ride the bikes if you want. You will have to share for now. Duncan can show you the trails later if you want to look around. There's a rec room downstairs next to Duncan's room, where you can watch TV after homework and chores are done. Everyone has a few chores. There's a lot to do in a family and now there are more of us. We all have to help out."

That evening, the new family sits together for a meal of roast chicken, fresh garden vegetables, and homemade dinner rolls. Eddie is given some chicken scraps in the corner.

After dinner, Samuel and Jonah clean up, and Mary shows Lisa two large, colourful tapestries to pick from, one with a lotus flower and the other a blue and green tie-dye. They take the fabric to the girls' room and contemplate decorating options.

When the kitchen is back in order, the boys retire to the living room. Jonah plays a tune on the guitar and Samuel starts a fire in the stove. The boys laugh and make jokes with Jonah. Jonah passes the guitar to Duncan.

"Let's hear what you've been working on."

Duncan takes the guitar and begins strumming his latest version of "I Walk the Line."

Samuel teases his brother. "Sounds like you're torturing a cat! I don't think those lessons are working, Dad."

Jonah makes a funny face, confirming his secret agreement with Samuel.

"It takes time. You can't become a Johnny Cash or a Jonah Marcel over night."

Samuel rolls his eyes and mumbles under his breath. "A Jonah Marcel, maybe."

Duncan ignores his brother's comments and continues to strum loudly. "Da da da dada da, hmm, hmm, hmm."

"Maybe it would help if you sang the actual words, Duncan." Jonah winks.

Samuel shoots him a look of distress. "Oh, right, increase the torture," he says.

"OK, Samuel, your brother is trying his best. You can go downstairs if you don't want to listen. Jonathan, do you know how to play?"

"No, sir," says Jonathan.

"You can call me Jonah if you like, Jonathan. Have you ever tried?"

"No, never," he says.

"Would you like to give it a go?" Duncan offers him the guitar. Jonathan looks like he's being handed an infant.

"Go ahead," says Jonah. "I can teach you three basic chords."

Jonathan takes the guitar and holds it the way he has seen other people hold it. It feels strange. Hollow. He has never thought about holding one, or even imagined why he would want to.

Duncan shows him where to place his fingers and tells him to press hard on the strings. "Now strum," he says.

Jonathan rubs his hand over the strings in an awkward downward stroke.

"Not quite," says Jonah. "Duncan, give him a pick."

Duncan hands him the pick and shows him how to hold it. "Firm, but light," he says. He physically adjusts Jonathan's fingers. "That's G. Now press in a bit and strum. Firm, but light."

Jonathan presses his fingers in the awkward position and strums again. This time the guitar hums a perfect G.

"That's it," says Jonah. "That's a G. Try it again."

Jonathan smiles and strums the G. He strums it again and again. He likes the sound. "Will you show me another one?" he asks.

Duncan laughs. "He's hooked already," he says.

Samuel runs into the kitchen for a snack and hears the new student. "Oh no," he moans. "What are you doing?"

"Never you mind, Samuel," says Jonah. "We have you outnumbered."

Samuel retreats downstairs again.

Duncan shows Jonathan the C and D chords, allowing the strings to vibrate their unique sound. "Listen, hear the difference? This is C and this is D. Now watch how my fingers change. Hum, hum, hum..."

They take turns on the guitar. Duncan plays Johnny Cash, minus the lyrics, and Jonathan practices the three chords while Jonah snores in the La-Z-Boy. Mary tucks in the two girls, then ushers the boys to bed.

"Jonathan and Lisa have a big day tomorrow, at a new school. It's time for bed."

Jonathan settles into his bed in his new room and attempts to sleep. His fingertips feel numb and a little sore from pressing the strings, but he is grateful for the distraction. Their first day with the Marcel family was better than expected. It was fun. Easy.

His new bed is more comfortable than his last and the bedding smells fresh.

Despite the good start, something keeps him from sleeping. He tosses and turns like the waves on Rosie Bay, his mind filled with questions. He wonders how much Jonah and Mary know about the assault on Nora Beach. Who do they expect him to be? He must start over again, attend community gatherings, learn the traditions, meet with Daiji, and volunteer for Stamer.

He must be the boy everyone expects him to be—a boy worthy of second chances.

George Jr.

The Nootka School sits on a scenic hill in Conuma. The ten-acre parcel is on the most elevated ridge in town, offering striking views of the valley and a network of cobalt-coloured rivers below. Its southwest location is blessed with sun most of the day, filtered through a forest of Sitka spruce and cedar. The building itself is shaped like an L, housing the elementary and primary grades on one side, and junior and senior grades on the other.

Lisa is happy to have Lilly as her personal tour guide on her first day. Mary has arranged for the girls to be in the same class. The class size is much smaller than she is used to, and her teacher, Ms. Warner, assigns Lisa a seat at Lilly's table. The students are already aware of her arrival and spent Friday's art class preparing a colourful welcome sign in her honour. Lisa's worries disappeared overnight, thanks to the thoughtful accommodations and, as she sees it, the help of the lotus flower of courage hanging above her bed. Whatever the source of her contentment, Mary is relieved to see such a promising adjustment.

Jonathan is in neither Samuel nor Duncan's grade, but falls in between the two—a position Jonah is sure will work to everyone's advantage. Jonathan has decided not to be overly concerned about his first day by reminding himself he's had plenty of change in his life. Nootka is much smaller than the school in Ramsey and doesn't appear to be as threatening as any of his previous experiences.

Jonathan presents as bit of a mystery to his classmates. His stoic presence is easily mistaken for quiet confidence, leaving onlookers to ponder.

Jonathan's teacher, Mr. Wick, assigns him to an empty seat second from the back. Jonathan walks to the desk, retrieves a pen and paper from his pack, and settles in for English One. He's only there for a minute when he becomes distracted by a putrid smell. The indescribable sourness wafts into his nostrils, making him gag.

He looks around for the source of the smell and catches the eye of the girl sitting across from him. She covers her nose with her sleeve and, with a look of disgust, points to a spot below Jonathan's desk. In a panic, Jonathan looks under his feet, expecting to see a smelly turd stuck to his shoe, but to his relief, he discovers his shoes are clean. He quickly checks the bottom of his backpack but does not find the source.

The young girl is still pointing below his desk, muffling her laughter and shaking her head. In his struggle to check his shoes again, Jonathan bumps the shoeless feet of the student behind him. They are leisurely stretched out under Jonathan's desk, and covered with blown out, dingy grey socks. He's found the source of the stench.

He looks directly behind him to see George Jr. Blakely, who is slumped so low in his desk that the backrest sits at his neck. George is lavishing himself with a quick nap, oblivious to the horror his grey socks are creating.

Jonathan looks at the pretty young girl again who has also been subjected to the stinky sock assault. She hands him a note that reads *George Jr. Stinkbomb*! Jonathan quickly scribbles back *Do you have a plan of attack*? The young girl gives an unexpected laugh, but then quickly straightens up to avoid detection.

Luckily, the bell rings and they all race from their seats. Jonathan hopes to speak with his new conspirator outside the classroom, but she joins her two friends, who are eagerly waiting for her outside the door.

At lunchtime, Jonathan goes outside to join Duncan, who is sitting with a few friends. Duncan introduces him to the others. They are busy talking about their idiot math teacher, who has an affinity for pop quizzes.

"You'll have Martin next year," says Duncan. "He's the only level two math teacher."

"Something to look forward to," says Jonathan. He tells Duncan about the sock assault in his last class and Duncan explodes into laughter.

"Don't tell my mom," says Duncan. "She'll come in with new socks for sure."

"I might have to, then," says Jonathan. The two boys burst into laughter again.

"Sock assault. That's funny," says Duncan.

"No, it's not! It's really not!" says Jonathan. He points to the trees. "That's him."

"Where?" asks Duncan.

"Over there, walking into the woods. Where's he going? Looks like he's leaving."

"Oh, that guy," says Duncan. "That's George Jr."

"Yes, that's the guy," says Jonathan.

"George Jr. is a bit strange. He gets into trouble a lot."

"What kind of trouble?" asks Jonathan.

"I don't know," says Duncan. "All kinds. He may need more than just socks. Look, I have to go. I have another quiz this afternoon. It's a crazy week. I'll see you at home, OK?"

"Yup," says Jonathan.

Jonathan leaves the explanation at that, sensing there's more to George Jr. than he understands.

That evening, the family sits together for dinner and discusses the events of the day. Lilly tells everyone about the beautiful welcome sign her class made for Lisa. Lisa leaves the table, runs to her room, and returns, proudly displaying the poster.

"That's so lovely!" says Mary. "So you like your class, then?"

"Yes. Ms. Warner is very nice, and I sit at Lilly's table most of the time, except for math, when we go to Mrs. Andrews' class. She wants me to get to know other students."

"Well, that's OK," says Mary. "How was your day, Jonathan?"

"It was fine," says Jonathan, filling his mouth with more beef stew.

"Jonathan was assaulted!" says Duncan.

"What do you mean, assaulted?" asks Mary.

Jonah stops chewing and appears to freeze in place. Jonathan and Duncan begin laughing.

"What's so funny?" asks Samuel.

"By socks," says Jonathan, trying not to spit out his mouthful of potato.

"What happened?" says Mary, getting impatient.

Duncan continues to laugh while Jonathan swallows and tries to regain his composure.

"It was George Jr.," says Duncan. "And his socks."

"OK, you two are not making any sense at all," says Mary. She gets up to refill the water jug.

"Duncan and Jonathan, you must explain yourself, please," says Jonah.

Duncan tells the story of the stinky socks. The children all laugh at the stink bomb in Jonathan's class. Jonah even laughs at Jonathan's panic to check his shoes. Mary doesn't laugh. She bows her head and whispers to herself.

"What's wrong, Mom? You're going to buy him new socks, aren't you?" says Duncan.

"The poor child. It's not his fault his socks smell. You boys must not make fun of him. I will take care of this."

Jonah looks at Mary and nods. He knows his compassionate wife is making plans.

"OK, enough poking fun at poor George Jr.'s expense," says Jonah.

"I'm sorry, Mary," says Jonathan.

"It's OK, Jonathan," says Mary.

Lisa and Lilly help Mary clean up, and the boys help Jonah carry wood in from the shed. Then Mary instructs the children to attend to their homework and leaves for the general store.

Settling In

Jonathan's first month at Nootka is like stepping up to the start line when everyone else is halfway to the finish. He knew starting in the middle of the term would be hard. He's had to do it before. After meeting with all his teachers, he decides to do extra work at night to make up for lost time. His late start on *The Lord of the Flies* excludes him from the discussion in English class, but Mr. Wick estimates reading ten pages a night ought to get him up to speed in a timely manner.

At first, Jonathan thought it was a lot, but he soon finds himself immersed in the lives of the stranded boys. He often reads past his assigned pages to find out what happened next. He's fascinated by the adventure, and often compares the characters to himself and Jimmy and their time in the forest. He wonders how he and his brother would act if they were stranded on an island. He hopes they would be smart like Simon or Ralph, but knows things often go wrong. He is sure of one thing: He would want Jimmy on his side.

Jonathan becomes friends with Cathy, who sits across from him in English class and who introduced him to George Jr.'s feet. He learns that her mother works in the office. Cathy sings in the school choir and takes piano lessons. She is impressed that Jonathan is learning to play the guitar and trying not to sound like a tortured cat.

The stinky socks are a distant threat, as George Jr. is absent more than most and Mary asked him to "try not to make fun." George Jr.'s absence has helped Jonathan heed that request, but he can't help wondering what keeps George Jr. away. Maybe it has something to do with his early departure the other day, or maybe he realized he was the subject of their laughter. Jonathan finds himself pondering the life of George Jr. and his stinky feet more often than he expected.

One late October weekend, Jonah takes the children for a hike through the forest to find mushrooms. Samuel and Lilly help Jonathan and Lisa distinguish between a tasty chanterelle and a potential stomachache. Jonah steers them through the terrain, quizzing them on the trees and moss, while Duncan checks everybody's work before adding it to the valuable collection.

After several hours and a full basket, they have lunch at a favorite family spot under Old Red. Jonah explains that it is a sacred site where his great-grandfather would take his father to sit. It's one of the largest trees in the forest. Jonathan and Lisa have never seen such a giant. A tall cedar, estimated to be seven or eight hundred years old and over a hundred feet tall. It's the perfect sheltered location for a lunch of hot tea, sandwiches, and Mary's sugar cookies.

For the rest of the day, they make games out of naming birds and identifying animal tracks. The Marcel children could name almost every wildflower, fern, and moss in the forest, and Jonah makes everyone keep a close eye on the sky.

"There's no excuse for getting caught in bad weather," he says.

Jonathan and Lisa are beginning to love their new home. It isn't just the genuine caring in the family, but something else. Jonathan sensed it from Lisa after she came looking for him one night before bed. She found him petting Eddie on the deck behind the house.

"Why are they always smiling?"

She posed the question as if the behavior was odd or suspicious.

"What do you mean?" he asked her.

"Lilly is always laughing and smiling with Mary. Samuel and Duncan too. What's so funny?"

It wasn't until much later that Jonathan realized the confusion in his young sister's observation. It wasn't the smiling and laughing that was odd, but how their behavior and emotions contrasted so starkly with her own. While he didn't know how to answer her at the time, he knew she was having difficulty trusting her new life. She was frightened someone would rip it out from under her at any time. A feeling he understood as well. There was lightness to their new family, a trust they shared that was always present.

Maybe, with time, he and Lisa would feel it too.

Volunteering

By the end of term, Jonathan has managed to catch up to the rest of the grade eight students. He excels in English, partly due to a highly relatable novel and partly because of his new best friend, Cathy. The two became obsessively close, studying, taking walks, and spending every spare hour together. Their close bond became such a concern to the adults that Jonah was forced to have "the talk" with Jonathan. Jonathan smiled and thanked Jonah while secretly wanting to die of embarrassment. Mary and Jonah were confident they had prepared the children for all the stages of life, but both were secretly grateful for Jonathan's tight schedule.

School and social activities were only part of Jonathan's week. Jonah drove him to Ramsey to volunteer at Stamer's law office most Friday afternoons, except during exams. He was given a free period at the end of the school week to leave early. Jonathan enjoyed his time at Stamer's office and endeavoured to understand what seemed to be the extremely complex system of law.

At the end of the fall term, during Christmas break, Jonathan agreed to spend a couple of afternoons at Stamer's office. On Monday, he would help organize files and mail letters, and on Friday, he would help Stamer's secretary, Nancy, make a list of special requests.

Jonathan liked Fridays the most. Fridays were court days for Stamer, and while he was away, Jonathan and Nancy would arrange his pro bono cases in order of priority. Nancy would gather all the calls, messages, and drop -ins from the week and compile them into a special request list that Jonathan was in charge of. The names were submitted by probation officers, social workers, and desperate mothers who viewed Stamer as "their only hope." Nancy would tell Jonathan whether to add the name to the list or not. Jonathan kept the list and would write the address and phone numbers next to the names.

In the afternoon, Nancy and Jonathan would present the list to Stamer, making a case for the top five. Stamer would make adjustments and the top five would receive letters informing them of their appointment times.

Nancy would explain to Stamer who had most urgent need, or, as Jonathan saw it, who was in the most trouble with the least amount of hope. Jonathan suspected his name was on the special request list at some point. Stamer would listen to Nancy present each case and, at times, ask Jonathan if he agreed. Jonathan always did, as he trusted that Nancy had a better grasp on the criteria. She seemed to be the type of lady who would never find herself on such a list, which he figured made her credible. He was grateful to be asked all the same.

This Friday afternoon, Jonathan is busy getting the list ready for Stamer when a woman from Conuma comes in. Jonathan recognizes her face, but can't remember where he's seen her before. She looks nervous and worried, like most of the faces that come in. Nancy is busy on the phone, so the woman quietly takes a seat in the waiting area.

As soon as Nancy puts down the phone, a social worker named Stacey comes in with an older kid. Jonathan has seen them before. She is from Ramsey and always smiles at Jonathan. She tells Nancy they are supposed to be meeting Stamer in court. Nancy takes them to the back room and Stacey explains to Nancy why they aren't at the courthouse. Jonathan can tell something is wrong. Someone didn't show up, is afraid, or changed their mind about something.

Nancy dials Stamer at the courthouse to tell him there's a problem. Things get pretty hectic, and Nancy looks concerned. Amid the chaos, the quiet woman leaves without speaking to anyone. Jonah comes to pick up Jonathan and he leaves without telling Nancy about the woman.

The following Monday, Jonathan is putting letters into envelopes and preparing them for the post office when he sees the familiar lady enter the office again. He can see that Nancy is already busy helping several other people. Jonathan wonders what's happening with the woman. It must be important enough to make the drive from Conuma to Ramsey at least twice that he's seen. He wants to tell her that it's best to come on Fridays, but understands it's Nancy's job to talk to the clients, not his. After a while, the woman leaves again.

Later that day, Jonah comes by to pick Jonathan up on his way back from town.

"How is Chris today?" asks Jonah.

Jonathan doesn't answer. He's thinking about the quiet woman and how they weren't able to see her. She doesn't seem to have time to wait. He wonders what's bothering her—then, suddenly, he remembers! He knows where he's seen her. It was at the principal's office. She's George Jr.'s mother! He saw her in the office with George Jr. after he got in trouble for calling the teacher a dumb twit. Jonathan remembers the woman because she has the same worn out and sad look that she had that day in the principal's office.

Why did she come? Is it about George Jr.? What did he do this time?

"Jonathan, are you OK?" asks Jonah. "Did you hear me?"

"What did you say?" asks Jonathan.

"I asked if you had a hard day at the office."

Jonathan smiles. "No, I'm OK. Just a little tired."

"I think you are tired. I made a good joke and you missed it!"

Jonathan laughs again. "Maybe you need a break from some of this volunteer work. It's almost Christmas."

"I will, Jonah. After Friday, the office closes for two weeks."

"Good," says Jonah. "We have to get a Christmas tree on Saturday."

The List

Jonathan can barely wait to get up on Friday morning and volunteer at Stamer's office. He's been planning all night what he'll do if George Jr.'s mother comes back. He'll tell Nancy she's been in twice before, but they were just too busy to talk to her and she really needs help. George Jr. often gets into trouble with the teachers and there's no telling what's he done this time. Mary would want him to try to help.

The Friday before Christmas turns out to be even busier than most Fridays. Jonathan is writing down all the names and phone numbers that Nancy has compiled and puts them in order according to Nancy's instructions. Nancy has a meeting in the boardroom with a family that finally reached the top of the list after weeks of waiting.

"It's the Christmas rush," she says. "When people know we're going to be closed for two weeks, they panic. They want to state their case so they can rest easy for the holiday. Jonathan, I need you to answer the phones while I'm busy. I talked to Stamer about it and he said it was OK. If we let them all go to the answering machine, we'll never get through them all."

"OK," says Jonathan. "I will."

Nancy writes on a piece of paper exactly what she wants Jonathan to say so he doesn't forget. Jonathan doesn't need to look at the paper. He's heard it a hundred times. "Good day, Stamer Law Office. Mr. Stamer is in court today. Can I take a message?"

He's not to answer any questions. He's just supposed to take a message, and Nancy will call them back as soon as she can. One person on the phone sounds like he's desperate.

"Can you please ask her to call me back today? It's very important," he says.

Jonathan notices that everyone sounds desperate. He decides to make another list rating the urgency of the messages. He's relieved when Nancy finishes her meeting and returns to her post as gatekeeper of the messages.

Nancy looks confused when she sees the triaging of the phone messages and thanks him for his effort.

By the time they meet with Stamer at the end of the day, Jonathan realizes George Jr.'s mother didn't come back. Maybe she gave up. Now she won't rest easy for the holidays.

Stamer goes over their list of requests, remarking that it's a particularly long one and they will all have to wait until the new year.

"Jonathan, is there anything you would like to say about the list?" Stamer asks.

Jonathan pauses. Then, to everyone's surprise, he has something to add: "Yes. I think there's someone else who should be on it."

Nancy stops packing her bag and looks at Jonathan, curious about the addendum.

"There's a woman who came in twice this week, but we didn't have time to talk to her."

"Oh," says Nancy. "What woman was that?"

"It wasn't anyone's fault," he says. "Nancy was busy with the social worker and the woman didn't wait long before leaving. She did it twice."

"Yes, I understand, Jonathan. That happens sometimes. Nancy is very busy out here. Tell us why you think she should be on the list. Do you know her name?"

"Yes, she's from Conuma. She's George Jr.'s mother. I've seen her at my school."

Nancy smiles and sits back down. "Do you know the last name?" she asks.

"No, but I can find out. Mary knows."

"Why do you think this woman needs to be on the list?" asks Stamer.

Jonathan thinks for a moment. The stinky socks wouldn't be a good reason to be on Stamer's list. In fact, he doesn't really know the reason. He just knows George Jr. is in trouble and needs Stamer's help.

"I'm not sure why, but she most likely has an urgent need."

Stamer covers his mouth with his hand, hiding his smile.

Jonathan continues. "I know they don't have any money. George Jr. doesn't even have proper socks."

"Oh," says Nancy.

Stamer rubs his chin and looks at his list. "OK, Jonathan. Perhaps we can put George Jr. right after the Harris case. That's number six on the list. If you find out more over the holidays, or George Jr.'s mother decides to come back in, we will consider holding that spot for her. Thank you for bringing this to our attention. We will discuss it on our first Friday back."

"Sounds like a plan," says Nancy.

"Are you good with that, Jonathan?"

"Yes, thank you," he says.

Stamer shakes his hand. "Good work, Jonathan. I will see you in the new year."

When Jonah pulls into the parking lot, Jonathan is all smiles. He carries a gift wrapped in Christmas paper.

"What do you have there?" asks Jonah.

"It's from Mr. Stamer. He gave Nancy one too. She has a basket with all sorts of candy and wine and stuff. Can I open it?"

"That's up to you, Jonathan. It's your gift. I don't see why not."

Jonathan unwraps the gift and finds a notepad in a brown leather folder, exactly like the one Stamer has. Engraved on the front of the soft leather are the words *Factis ut credam facis.* Jonathan opens the first page and recognizes Stamer's writing.

Thanks for all your help, Jonathan. It's been great having you around. Merry Christmas to you and your family! – Christopher Stamer

"That's a pretty fancy scribbler," says Jonah.

"It's just like Mr. Stamer's," says Jonathan. The notebook looks expensive. He runs his fingers over the words on the front. "I wonder what it means. *Factis ut credam facis.*"

"That's Latin," says Jonah. "The legal system uses a lot of Latin words. It's a carryover from Roman times. You'll have to look that one up. Mary may have an encyclopedia for you at home. That's a very nice gift. You'll have to use it for something special.

"We're getting a few snowflakes. Just in time for Christmas. Lilly and Lisa are excited about picking a Christmas tree tomorrow. Do you have much experience with trees?"

"No," says Jonathan.

"It will be fun, then," says Jonah.

"Yes," says Jonathan. "What kind of tree will work best?"

"I think a fir tree does the best job. There are lots of them where we had our picnic, remember?

Jonathan thinks it will be fun to pick out a tree with the others and decorate it.

"Can we put popcorn on the tree?" asks Jonathan.

"Well, what would a tree be without popcorn?" says Jonah.

Later that evening, Jonathan learns from Mary that George Jr.'s last name is Blakely.

"Why do you want to know?" asks Mary.

"I thought I saw his mother at Mr. Stamer's office, but I'm not supposed to talk about who comes in, so please don't tell anyone," Jonathan says.

"I understand," says Mary. "I won't."

Mary helps Jonathan find the meaning of the words that are on the cover of his notepad. "*Factis ut credam facis*. Here it is," she says. "'No need of words, trust deeds,'" says Mary. "Or, more commonly, 'actions speak louder than words.' Yes, that's a good one, Jonathan."

Jonathan goes to bed contemplating the meaning of *factis ut credam facis*. Tomorrow is Saturday. After he picks a tree with his family, he will see Daiji. He will tell him about his gift. Jonathan barely finishes this thought before he falls fast asleep.

Family Time

On Saturday morning, Lisa wakes Jonathan. "Jonathan, you have to get up. We need to get a tree. Everyone else is awake."

Jonathan sits up straight in bed, alarmed. "Are they waiting for me?" he asks.

"Yes. Well, Samuel and Duncan are still having breakfast, but Jonah wants to leave soon. Isn't it exciting, Jonathan?"

"Yes, yes, very exciting, Lisa. I'll be right there."

"I've never picked out a Christmas tree before. Have you, Jonathan?"

"Lisa, go downstairs! I'll be there soon." Lisa leaves him so he can get dressed. He looks at the clock on Samuel's table. It's nine-thirty. He can't believe he slept so long. He quickly shovels a bowl of cereal into his belly and joins the others in Jonah's truck.

Mary yells from the porch.

"Make sure it's not too big and has branches all around. No bare spots!"

Jonah drives them to a forest road, where some of the local loggers have been cutting.

"We'll take a tree from here," says Jonah. "There looks to be some nice firs over there."

The children investigate a few potentials, keeping Mary's words in mind.

"Too skimpy," says Samuel.

"This one is full," Lilly says, pointing to a pine.

"Pines dry out quickly and their needles make a mess. I don't think your mom wants a pine," says Jonah.

"How about this one?" asks Duncan. "It's full enough and I don't see any holes."

The five children walk around the tree, surveying every inch of it.

"I think that will work. And they smell the best," says Jonah.

Everyone agrees on the full, healthy, smells-like-Christmas fir tree. Jonah cuts down the tree and the boys drag it to the truck. They decide to toast their success with the hot chocolate Jonah brought in the thermos before they all pile back into the truck.

Two hours later, they return home with a fir that seems to fit all of Mary's requirements. Duncan helps Jonah straighten the tree in the stand and Lilly gets the water jug. Lisa sits on the floor with her two legs tucked under her, staring up at the Christmas tree while Samuel tries to untangle the lights. Mary calls Jonathan into the kitchen.

"Jonathan, I think I know why you saw Mrs. Blakely at Stamer Law Office."

"Why?" asks Jonathan. "Is George Jr. in trouble?"

"No, it's not George Jr. It's his older brother, Malcolm. I know Malcolm. He works at the general store. He's not a bad kid, he just hangs out with the wrong crowd and has no one to look up to. Maisy, his mother, works at the diner during the day and cleans the schools at night. Their dad left a couple of years ago. She barely has time to take care of George Jr., so I'm sure Malcolm does whatever he wants. She tells me Malcolm usually helps out at home with George Jr., but lately, he's been coming in late. Someone broke into the general store and they are blaming it on Malcolm. He swears he didn't do it, but he's been charged. She told me she's been going to the law office in between her two jobs, hoping Christopher can help, but she says she hasn't been able to stay long enough to see him. Do you think Christopher will help?"

"I think so," says Jonathan. "If you can give me her phone number, she will stay on our list. Mr. Stamer said if I got more information, he might be able to help."

Jonah comes into the kitchen to make the popcorn. "What are you two in cahoots about?"

Jonathan looks at Mary, concerned.

"Oh, nothing," she says. "Jonathan has never put popcorn on a tree before."

"You haven't? I thought you were the one who asked to put popcorn on the tree," says Jonah.

"I do," he says. "I saw it before. I just don't know how it's done."

"Oh, well!" says Jonah. "We will soon fix that."

Jonathan checks the time. "I'll help when I get back. I have to see Daiji."

"That's today?" asks Jonah.

"Yes, it's our last meeting for a couple of weeks. It's just down the road at the band office. I can walk from here."

Daiji

Jonathan is excited. He arrives at the band office and tells the secretary, Marsha, he is here to see Daiji. Marsha smiles and hands him a piece of paper folded in half with his name on it. Jonathan opens the note and reads: *I'm outside with Conuma.*

Jonathan smiles and thanks Marsha. He heads outside and looks around the grounds. The band office sits on a lush acre of cedar trees, rimmed by the watchful Conuma Peak. Daiji always finds it difficult to be inside during Jonathan's visits.

Jonathan can see his mentor in the distance, sitting in the gazebo. He's dressed warmly in a white coat and hat that one of the elders made from home-spun wool. The late afternoon sun sits low in the sky, casting a warm pink glow on the majestic peak. Miniature ice crystals float in the air and shimmer silver and blue in the sun. Jonathan walks to the gazebo and sits next to Daiji to share the view.

"Will you climb her some day?" asks Daiji.

"Conuma Peak?"

"Yes."

"Jonah says it's difficult, but people have done it. So yes, maybe I will."

"I think it would be a worthwhile journey," says Daiji.

"Maybe we should climb together?" says Jonathan.

Daiji smiles, contemplating the possibility. "How was your week?"

"I have been working with Mr. Stamer this week."

"That must be interesting. What did you learn there?"

"Well, I guess I learned that Mr. Stamer helps a lot of people, especially those with urgent need."

Daiji nods. "I expect there are a lot of those people."

"Yes, there are."

"You are very fortunate to have the opportunity to learn from Christopher. He is a good person."

"Yes, I know." Jonathan looks far away.

"What's on your mind, Jonathan?"

"Why do some of us get to live in good homes, where everyone laughs and smiles, while others live in homes where they never see their parents? Where their mom has to work two jobs and their dad has left them, and then they get into trouble, or they have no parents at all and they're alone. It just isn't fair."

Daiji touches his thoughtful student on the shoulder. "Yes, Jonathan, that is a good question indeed. Many people suffer for years, generations, or lifetimes and carry pain in their hearts. There is a heavy energy that lives inside them. They stay angry and believe the struggle is all they have. They complain and react to everyone in anger. It becomes the ordinary and familiar way of doing things. They expect life to be hard, and so it is. Sometimes they try to escape it by drinking too much or using drugs. Eventually, some people become tired of the weight and decide they have carried it long enough. They step out of the old energy of complaints and reach for the exception—a new way of seeing and behaving in the world."

"How do you do that?" asks Jonathan. "How do you get rid of the bad energy?"

"Well, Jonathan, first you have to understand that everyone chooses the path that's right for them. It's the path you need to be on to learn, to face the challenges that will awaken you to the truth. This is what our journey is about. It's important to understand that you can change your path and awaken anytime you want, but it's not your job to change someone else's path.

"Here, we can only be kind. We can offer those who struggle empathy, compassion, acceptance, and forgiveness. When we inject them with love and acceptance, it awakens them for a moment—and it awakens you as well. Your life becomes lighter, happier, more on track. Your energy moves with the positive flow of life, and good things happen. You begin to enjoy all the moments that you have. Things slow down. You create in a conscious way.

"But don't take my word for it. Practice it yourself. Notice how you feel the next time you accept someone for who they are or what they are going through, and offer them compassion instead of judgment."

Jonathan is quiet, contemplating every word.

"I suspect you understand this already, Jonathan," Daiji says.

"Do you know the expression 'actions speak louder than words'?" asks Jonathan.

"Yes, Jonathan, and so do you. Sometimes we know in our hearts what needs to be done, and we act. We don't need to discuss it with others or make promises. We just act out of the wisdom of our hearts. Why do you ask?"

"Mr. Stamer gave me a notepad with those words in Latin."

Daiji smiles and lowers his eyes. "Yes, of course. Christopher can see your special gift."

"I have something for you," says Jonathan. He takes a small package from his pocket, wrapped in Christmas paper covered with red glitter and stars. "Lisa made the paper."

"It's beautiful." Daiji smiles and unwraps the gift.

"I made it in my cultural arts class. It's not as good as yours. It's a whale, like the one you showed us on Nora Beach. I still have that one," Jonathan says.

"Well, now we both have one," says Daiji. "Thank you, Jonathan. And this is for you."

Daiji hands him a square box wrapped in paper. Jonathan opens the box and finds a book. On the cover is a wolf and a shaman dressed in regalia.

"It's stories about our ancient traditions, some of the same stories my father shared with me. I hope you enjoy reading them."

"Thank you, Daiji. I will read them over Christmas."

"Enjoy your family, Jonathan. Enjoy your good fortune, living and sleeping under Conuma Peak. Enjoy this path. I think it's an important one for you."

Jonathan returns home to find the Christmas tree decorated with sparkling, coloured lights, bright red and gold ornaments, silver tinsel, and popcorn garland. Eddie is tucked underneath the bottom branches and Jonah is playing the guitar.

"Isn't it the most beautiful tree you've ever seen?" asks Lisa.

"Yes, it is," says Jonathan.

"You missed making the popcorn garland," says Lilly.

"You missed eating the popcorn garland!" says Samuel.

"We saved you the star," says Lisa. "You have to plug it into the lights on the top."

Mary puts the step stool next to the tree and hands Jonathan the golden star. Jonathan places it on top, like he's crowing a king. He connects it to the rest of the lights. The star shines from the top of the tree, casting a golden glow. Jonathan notices everyone watching him, faces shining and smiling. Even Eddie takes a pause from his grooming to look up at Jonathan.

"Exceptional!" says Jonah.

"Merry Christmas," says Lisa. She smiles at her brother and quickly wipes her eyes.

A New Friend

The first day back to school is hectic. Jonathan's teachers present the curriculum outcomes for the term, complete with scheduled tests, required readings, and books the students must borrow from the library. Jonathan is interested in learning about the new novel for English class, and is disappointed to discover poetry will be the focus for the rest of the year.

He and Cathy have taken their regular seats across from each other when they notice George Jr. approaching. Cathy can't hide her disappointment when he picks the seat behind Jonathan. Cathy quickly scans the class and notices two other seats on the other side of the room.

"Let's go," she says to Jonathan. "I want to sit by the window."

Jonathan understands Cathy's sudden attachment to the window seat but has something else in mind. "Nah, that's OK. I want to stay here."

Cathy gives him a disapproving look.

Jonathan turns around in his desk. "Hello, George. How were your holidays?"

George is startled by the question. He clears his throat and sits up straight. "Pretty good," he says.

"Glad to hear it," says Jonathan.

Jonathan notices how simple it is to talk to George Jr. and how surprised he is to hear his voice. Jonathan doesn't remember hearing George Jr. speak before and decides to keep talking to him every day. He soon finds himself looking forward to talking with George Jr. It turns out he has quite a sense of humor, and he and Jonathan enjoy quoting the poem of the week. George Jr. can quote entire passages.

"'The flames just soared, and the furnace roared—such a blaze you seldom see; and I burrowed a hole in the glowing coal, and I stuffed in Sam McGee.'"

Cathy even chuckles when, out of the blue, before taking his seat, he looks at her and proclaims, "Shall I compare thee to a summer's day?"

The three students burst into laughter and have to be brought back to order by a curious Mr. Wick, who can't help but notice a revived George Jr.

George and Jonathan spend their lunch breaks together and decide to join the soccer team. Mary and Jonah are surprised when George turns up on the weekends and stays for supper, but the family delights in his eagerness to make them laugh, and welcomes him with open arms.

Jonathan soon learns that George Jr.'s brother, Malcolm, was in trouble for a while, but with the help of a good lawyer in Ramsey, he was proven innocent and has settled down considerably. Jonathan pretends he knows nothing about it. Malcolm now works at the grocery store full time and is going to college next year.

Jonathan can't help but be bewildered by the turn of events in George Jr.'s life. He discusses it with Daiji, who advises him not to ponder the good fortune too closely, but to simply enjoy the moments he spends with George Jr., which Jonathan does. An unexpected friendship is something to be thankful for.

Jonathan

By Jonathan's sixteenth birthday, his contractual obligations with the Nuu-chah-nulth Nation are long over, but his vision for the future is just gaining focus. He excels in high school, graduates with honours, and works for Stamer as a student during the summer months.

Over the years, Stamer's attention has broadened to the political arena, and he secured a federal seat for the Ramsey district, representing a progressive new political party calling for social reform. He has pushed for new policies on environmental protection, and has often found himself going head-to-head with the burgeoning oil and gas sector. He is a minority voice in an economy-focused arena, which has only strengthened his resolve to bring balance to competing priorities. He never misses an opportunity to highlight the high cost of building a limitless economy at the expense of environmental responsibility.

Jonathan has joined Chris at several heated protests on proposed new projects, demanding that environmental assessments and First Nation discussions take place before a single rock is turned. His developing interest in a legal career has been a natural progression, and Stamer is more than happy to help get him there.

Jimmy

January mornings can be wet and windy on the northern coast.

Jimmy takes his last slices of ham and cheese, stuffs them between two pieces of buttered bread, and wraps it all up with foil. He tosses it in his pack along with an apple and two chocolate chip cookies saved from last night's takeout. His roommate, Glen, snores loudly on the couch. Jimmy waits outside for his ride to avoid waking the irritable man, who never misses an opportunity to remind him how lucky he is to get a room at such a good price downtown.

"If you're a real man, you'll have the rent on time," Glen always says, ritually, a few days before Jimmy's payment is due. It got old the second month in. Strong words from a man whose only job seems to be figuring out how to pay for his next case of beer and keeping his cable from being cut off.

Jimmy raises his collar around his neck, looking for some protection from the damp air. He came north for work, but longs to return to Uncle Bernie's cabin on the island. His plan is to do high-paying labour for a few months and retreat back to the wilderness for the rest of the year.

His stomach burns from the straight shots he knocked back with Glen before bed. He lights a cigarette and takes a few long drags before he finally hears the old Bronco rattle toward him and stop.

"Hey, man," Tim says, clearly struggling with the early hour.

"Hey. We're going to be late. I can't lose this job," says Jimmy.

"Fuck 'em. We punch a full day. Who else are they going to find to do this crap labour?"

"I don't want Jones coming down on me. I just want to do my job and go home," says Jimmy. "You know what I mean?"

"It will be fine, Jim, relax. Jones doesn't even make it to the dock until noon."

Tim worked his way into receiving after a year on the dock and helped Jimmy get on as a labourer. They met at the Tap, the local bar, when Jimmy first arrived in town. Jimmy was cleaning tables, barely old enough to be working there. He and Tim began to talk, and Tim agreed to try to get him on as a gopher at the loading dock. They discovered that Jimmy lived on Tim's route, and Tim offered to pick him up in the mornings to help him out. Trouble is, Tim has a hard time getting to work on time.

Tim pulls into the parking lot. Jimmy jumps out and tries to take his place on the dock without being noticed. He and Antonio have been paired up to unload one of the sea cans and Jimmy is forty-five minutes late.

"Jim, nice of you to join me," Antonio says. "You're supposed to be helping me. I've been unloading this fucking thing by myself."

"Sorry," he says. "Tim had car trouble. We'll catch up. Take a breather for an hour."

Antonio is an Italian who also migrated to the city in search of a profitable quick fix. He quickly earned the nickname Jackhammer because commentary is mind-numbing on the early shifts and his mouth is the most energetic part of his body.

Jimmy begins unloading the crates off the sea can, onto the fork, and over to the loading station. He works quickly to make up for the late start.

Antonio sits back on a crate and lights a cigarette. He complains so much in between the puffs that he sounds like he's inhaling helium.

"Car trouble again! That's the second time this week. Tim better replace that piece of shit before you're both out of a job! Or you should take the bus in if you know what's good for you. That guy is bad news, Jimmy."

Jimmy keeps his head down, focusing on loading the fork and transporting the cargo to the dock. Antonio continues with his streak of complaints, stopping and starting again as Jimmy moves in and out of earshot.

"You're on thin ice, man. If Jones catches on, you'll be yanked, Jimmy."

Jimmy's getting tired of Antonio's relentless drivel. He remembers his ear protection, slaps on his muffs, and breathes a sigh of relief. He smiles on the inside, giving Antonio an occasional nod.

By the end of his shift, Jimmy has unloaded the entire can himself while Antonio sleeps between stacks of crates. He meets Tim in parking.

"How did it go?" Tim asks.

"Had to listen to Antonio bitch all day and I unloaded an entire can while he talked himself to sleep, because I was an hour late."

"That guy's a moron," says Tim. "Let's stop at the Tap for a quick one."

Jimmy doesn't really have the stomach for it, but figures he needs some numbing after the day he's had. They pull into the Tap and find a table at the back.

The bar is packed with labourers like himself trying to squeeze a moment of relief into the day before starting all over again tomorrow. A ritual that bodes well for the local barkeep and main reason behind the dingy bar's robust sales.

Jimmy and Tim bullshit about how they work harder than anyone else in the yard, how dense their supervisor is, and how much money Old Samson, the frugal owner of the Tap, rakes in off the sweat of his clientele. Tim figures Samson should spruce up the bar to attract more patrons, especially the female kind.

At around the fifth beer, Tim usually whines about missed opportunities. "Samson will never do it. He's too tight. He's got no motivation, and why should he? He's doing too well with a dirty rag and a broom to spend any cash on a reno. People got no pride, Jim, that's the problem. If I owned this place, I would make it a working man's pub that people look forward to coming to, with live entertainment and a strip bar. I would clean up. Samson's got no pride."

"You could turn in that shit Bronco," says Jimmy, egging him on.

"Gets you where you need to go," Tim snaps back with wounded pride.

Three or four beers later, Tim is getting acquainted with Roxy, a lady who's new to the area, a sign for Jimmy that it's time to leave. He finishes his last beer and is reaching for his coat when he sees Tim pointing to him in the corner. One of Roxy's friends heads in his direction.

"Hello there," she says. "I'm Marley. Your friend Tim says I should keep you company."

Jimmy looks at Tim, who gives him a thumbs up as he's heading out the door with Roxy.

"I guess so," he says. He can already feel tomorrow's pain a good six hours early. "I've never seen you here before. Do you live around here?"

"No. I'm staying with Roxy, but I don't usually go out. What about you?"

"Me and Tim live in Fort Marin. We work at the docks."

"You working tomorrow?" she asks.

"Yup, if Tim can get us there on time," he says.

Marley orders them two more beers and they share a plate of fries. Jimmy realizes he hasn't eaten anything since the ham and cheese sandwich at lunch. He can barely keep himself from shoveling down the fries all by himself.

"You're hungry," says Marley. "I better watch my fingers."

They finish off the fries and Marley orders another for the road.

"Where are you going?" Jimmy asks.

"Your place," she says.

"OK," he agrees. With any luck, Glen has managed to find his way to his own bed this evening.

Lost Chances

Jimmy wakes up with a pounding head. He looks for his clock that's buried under a pile of clothes on the floor. It's eight in the morning.

"Shit."

He jumps up and puts on his pants. Marley is asleep and naked under the sheets. Jimmy tries to remember the night before, but nothing dampens the panic. He sees an empty, soggy takeout plate from the Tap and remembers a few scant details: *Fries to go, Tim and Roxy, Marley, we're so late, too late!*

Jimmy runs to the door and goes outside in his bare feet. He looks up and down Fifth Avenue, hoping for the sight of the old Bronco, but reality kicks in. It's not coming. Tim is nowhere to be found. Probably still with Roxy. They've messed up for the last time. He returns to his room and shakes Marley awake.

"Can you give me something for a headache?" she asks.

"I don't have anything. We have to go."

"What do you mean we have to go?" she asks.

"I'm late for work and my roommate won't let me have anyone over. We have to go."

"Screw him." She rolls over.

"Marley, we have to go. I've probably lost my job today. I can't lose my room."

Marley sits up and starts getting dressed. Jimmy digs out a shirt and socks, trying to be as quiet as possible. They leave the apartment and begin walking back to the Tap.

"Where are we going?" she asks.

"I have to talk to Tim. I'm going to see if his truck is still at the Tap. Maybe I can leave him a note or something."

Marley stops, digs a joint out of her pocket, and lights it. "Here," she says. "You need to chill."

"I don't need that right now. I need to get to work."

"When are you supposed to be there?" she asks.

"Now," says Jimmy. "We're supposed to start at eight."

"Well, you're late," she says.

Jimmy gives her a hard look but bites his tongue. They make it to the Tap and find Tim's truck, but no sign of Tim.

Jimmy is quiet. He feels his chest getting tight. He tries to take a few deep breaths, but it doesn't help. He bends over and tries to blow out through his mouth, but that doesn't work either. He can feel his heart thundering in his chest. His breathing has gone shallow and his throat is closing off.

"What's wrong with you?" asks Marley.

"I should be at work," he says. "Don't you understand that? I just lost my job, which means I won't be able to pay my rent in two weeks."

"Just calm down, Jimmy. You'll get another job."

"It was hard enough to get this one!"

He feels sick. He runs over to the side of the building and begins throwing up.

Marley leans against Tim's bronco and takes a drag on the joint. Jimmy sits on the cold ground and wipes his chin. It's a cold time of year to be homeless. What's he going to do now? His head hurts. He looks up and sees Tim and Roxy walking toward the Bronco. Jimmy pushes himself up and goes over to meet them.

"What happened, man? You were supposed to pick me up," he says.

"And I suppose you were ready and waiting for me?"

"I was at home. We just walked here to look for you."

"Well, I didn't make it. We didn't need that shit job anyway," says Tim.

"Oh really? How are you planning to pay your rent?" asks Jimmy. "'Cause I'm going to be homeless in two weeks."

"Don't worry about it. We'll find something," says Tim.

Tim says a dramatic goodbye to Roxy, while Jimmy looks away, annoyed. Marley glances at Jimmy, expecting the same, but gets a numb, distracted look instead.

"Bye," says Jimmy. He walks away from Marley and gets in the truck.

Marley shakes her head and walks away.

Tim gets in the Bronco and gives Jimmy a ride home. "That wasn't very polite," says Tim.

"I have more important things to worry about," says Jimmy.

"You got to learn to relax, kid. Give me a call tomorrow. We'll figure something out," he says.

Ben White

Jimmy calls Tim every day for a week with no response. He gets up at the same time every morning, packs a lunch, and leaves the apartment to keep Glen in the dark about his sudden joblessness. He walks the streets from morning until evening, checking with every local business owner and job site he can get to in one day.

Every day, he covers a different area, all with the same chatter playing over and over in his head: Tim's promise to get them on somewhere else isn't as easy as he thought. Maybe he could only get himself on and that's why he isn't answering the phone. He's a liar! He could at least answer the phone. He doesn't give a shit if Jimmy is homeless. He knows it's his fault and he can't face Jimmy. Jimmy didn't want to stop at the Tap; he just wanted to go home and get a good night's sleep. If only Antonio hadn't been mouthing off all day and stressing Jimmy out, he would've had the willpower to just go home.

Every evening, Jimmy gets home exhausted from covering so many miles and hearing the same rejections. "Not hiring, kid." He can't afford the bus and only has a few dollars left, which he rations out for one meal a day. He buys a bag of apples for his lunches and some oatmeal for the morning. When Glen offers him a beer, he just walks past him and goes to bed, only to do it all over again the next day. It's only a matter of time before he'll be living on the street. Glen has already picked up the scent, asking Jimmy what's wrong and telling him he looks depressed.

He has good reason to be depressed, but it makes no difference. It will only get worse on the street.

Two days before he figures he'll be kicked out on the street, he puts an apple in his pocket and starts his morning ritual. He makes one last trip down Fifth Avenue and onto Main to check in at some of the restaurants and bars on the strip.

At least it's a little warmer today. The sun is peeking out and winter is loosening its grip. Maybe he won't freeze to death at this time of year. He stops into The Family Diner to treat himself to a coffee for his walk down the strip. It's the cheapest in town. The owner of the diner hands Jimmy his coffee. Jimmy pours in some sugar, and without lifting his head, pitches his well-rehearsed line.

"Sir, you wouldn't be looking for any help in this fine diner of yours, would you?"

To his shock, the friendly man doesn't say no, but answers with a question. "I remember you. You asked me that last week. What can you do?"

Jimmy stops stirring the coffee, feeling a tiny glimmer of hope. He looks straight into the man's eyes.

"I can do anything you need me to do. I can clean, serve, whatever you need. I just really need a job."

"Well, I run this place by myself, but my wife keeps telling me I need help now that business has picked up. I need someone to work in the kitchen and make coffee and sandwiches. I make the specials and serve the customers, but I need someone to keep the small items going when it's busy and do odd jobs like clean the floors. I can give you forty hours a week, Monday to Friday. My wife helps out on Saturdays, and we are closed on Sundays. Do you think you can do that?"

"Yes, sir. I can do that no problem. I used to unload entire sea cans on the dock before I got laid off. I'm sure I can do whatever you need here."

"When can you start?"

"Now. I can start now."

"Come back tomorrow morning at eight. I can give you a schedule and show you what to do. What's your name?"

"It's Jimmy. Jimmy Richards."

"I'm Ben White. This is my diner. Nice to meet you." Ben extends his hand.

"Thank you, Mr. White. I will be here at eight tomorrow morning."

"See you then, Jimmy."

Jimmy takes his coffee and continues down the strip. He breathes a long, slow exhale. It's the first bit of relief he's felt in weeks. This is the break he needs. Forty hours a week will give him enough to pay for his room and a few groceries. He can easily walk here in thirty minutes. Glen never has to know the difference. After he pays his rent, he might tell him he decided to get a job closer, so he can walk and doesn't have to depend on a ride anymore.

Thank you, Mr. White.

The Family Diner

Jimmy is waiting outside the Family Diner at quarter to eight for Mr. White to arrive. He's down to his last apple and wondering if Mr. White will give him lunch. Surely if he's making the sandwiches, he can make one for himself too. That would help. It's a fine diner, with big windows. They will need to be cleaned often. This will be much easier than unloading sea cans. He won't get the same rate, but it will keep him off the street.

"Good morning, Jimmy," says Mr. White as he arrives.

Mr. White unlocks the door, and they go inside. He switches on the light and invites Jimmy into the back room. "You can leave your coat in here. You can use this room for your break and lunch. My office is in there; that's off-limits. That's where I do my paperwork. I want you to know honesty is very important to my wife and me. If you show me I can't trust you, I will let you go."

"I won't let you down," says Jimmy.

"Good. Glad to hear it. Come on, I'll show you the kitchen."

Mr. White shows Jimmy the coffee machine and instructs him to always have two full pots brewed. Then Mr. White makes a few sandwiches, showing Jimmy exactly how he likes them to be done. Jimmy makes a few more while Mr. White prepares the soup of the day. Mr. White's wife, Geena, drops in with two trays of fresh muffins, cinnamon rolls, and shortbread. She spends some time with Jimmy, pointing out all the appliances and how they operate.

"You have to clean the toaster oven tray after every shift, and maybe sooner if it's really busy. Rinse the coffee pots with a little vinegar at the end of the day, rinse again with water, and turn them upside down to keep them from getting too grimy."

Geena reminds him to wash his hands often and shows him the best way to load the dishwasher. Jimmy has never seen such a clean kitchen, and suspects Geena will expect the same from him.

His first Monday is a busy one. Mr. White prepares minestrone soup and a salad for the special of the day. He is out front serving customers while Geena helps Jimmy in the back, cuing and reminding when necessary.

By lunchtime, Jimmy figures he knows everything he needs to know about The Family Diner. As soon as the lunch rush is over, Mr. White tells him it's a good time to take his break.

"Do you mind if I make myself a sandwich?" asks Jimmy.

"No, no, just take one from the cooler," he says.

Jimmy takes an egg salad and mayo sandwich, one of Geena's muffins, and pours himself a coffee. He puts it on a tray and goes to the cash.

"It's OK, Jimmy," says Mr. White. Your lunch is free. It's a perk of working in our diner."

"Thank you, Mr. White," says Jimmy.

"Is that all you want? You can have some of the chef's salad, too, if you like."

Jimmy takes a plate of the chef's salad, then brings his lunch to the back. He hasn't had an egg and mayo sandwich or a salad in a while. He looks at his full tray and smiles. He takes his apple out of his coat pocket and puts it on the tray.

"Perfect. Fit for a king."

He savors every bite and finishes his entire lunch in ten minutes. He tells himself a free lunch and a short walk to work make up for the lower wage. He promises himself to do his very best at The Family Diner.

Welcomed Relief

Over the next two weeks, Jimmy learns the ins and outs of running a diner. He spends the mornings preparing sandwiches and coffee and does some chopping for the chef's salad. In the afternoons, he cleans the bathroom and kitchen floor. His first check comes in time to pay his room rent with a little left for groceries.

On Sunday, he has a beer with Glen and tells him about his new position at the diner. Glen knows the place. He used to go there for coffee when he worked at Value Furniture on the strip. He remembers the owner doing everything himself and figures he should have had help by now. Jimmy tells him that Mr. White says he's a natural in the kitchen and is allowing him to help prepare the sides. Glen advises that once Jimmy has been there a few months and is taking on more chores, he should ask for a raise. Jimmy figures free lunch is the only bonus he needs for now. He isn't rolling in dough, but he's not on the street.

Mr. White and Geena like his work, and on Fridays, Geena gives him some sweets to take home for himself and his roommate, much to Glen's delight.

"Did she say that?" Glen asks.

"That's what she said, Glen. A sweet for you and your roommate."

"Well, she sounds mighty sweet herself," he says.

Glen swoons over the cinnamon rolls and shortbreads like they were made just for him. Jimmy doesn't mind indulging him, especially since they correspond with a decrease in his dire warnings about being a man and having the rent on time.

Jimmy enjoys the weekends. He takes walks, reads the paper, and watches some baseball with Glen. He is happy the Whites trust him in the kitchen. He feels like a weight is lifting and that maybe he doesn't have to worry quite so much. Sometimes, while enjoying a walk in the park, he allows his mind to wander.

Perhaps I can have my own kitchen some day. If I learned everything there is to know this fast, how hard can it be? Maybe I will get a raise and save some money. It shouldn't be that hard, considering I'm walking to work and getting free lunches and snacks. I'll move out of this basement and have my own place.

Jimmy's mind feels lighter than it has for a long time. He wonders about his brother and sister—how they are, and if he will ever see them again.

An Acquaintance

Friday at the diner is busy. All the specials sell out and Jimmy is busy making extra sandwiches in the kitchen. He's about to run out of bread when Mr. White calls into back.

"Good job, Jimmy, I think the rush is over. We're winding down for the day. Give the floor a mop and I'll straighten out the kitchen," he says.

Jimmy goes to the back room to get the mop and fill the bucket.

He starts to clean the floor, hoping they won't get too many more customers, when he hears a familiar voice asking Mr. White for a coffee and sandwich. It's Tim! Jimmy looks up and there he is, dressed in work clothes, carrying his lunch basket, and ordering coffee. Jimmy's about to retreat to the back room when Tim looks up.

"Jimmy, hi," says Tim.

Jimmy doesn't know what to say. He stares at Mr. White, who is looking at him for a response.

"How are you? When did you start working here?" asks Tim, breaking the silence.

"Three months ago," says Jimmy.

"Well, come sit with me for a minute."

"I'm working. I have to clean up," says Jimmy.

"It's OK, Jimmy," says Mr. White. "I'll take care of the kitchen tonight. You talk to your friend."

Mr. White takes Jimmy's mop and bucket and moves into the kitchen. Jimmy takes a seat at the table across from Tim.

"What do you want, Tim? I really should be working. Mr. White has been very good to me."

"Yes, Ben is a good guy. I'm not going to keep you. I just want to apologize for not calling you. It's been rough. I just found work myself and had a lot going on. I knew you would be OK. Look at you! You're doing great."

"Thanks, Tim. Is that it? I have to go." Jimmy is about to stand when Tim grabs him by the arm. Jimmy stares at him. "What do you want?" he says quietly.

Mr. White catches Jimmy's eye and quickly turns away.

"Relax, Jimmy, I have to tell you something."

"Well, spit it out, then. The quicker you do that, the better."

"It's Marley."

"Marley? What about Marley? I haven't seen her since that night. I don't want to hear about Marley."

"Well, you might want to hear this."

Jimmy sits down. "What?"

"She's having a baby," says Tim.

Jimmy looks at Tim, confused and unsure why he is telling him this.

"Looks like you're going to be a dad, Jimmy."

Jimmy doesn't speak. He's deep in thought, wondering if such a thing is possible.

"Well, you look like you've seen a ghost, Jimmy," says Tim.

Mr. White calls from the kitchen, "Jimmy, we're going to close up now."

Jimmy looks at Tim, who seems to be enjoying Jimmy's discomfort. "I have to go," he says.

"I bet you do," says Tim. "We'll talk again soon. I'll tell Marley you said hi." He gets up from the table and shouts to Mr. White. "Thanks, Ben. See you around."

Jimmy walks to the kitchen to help Mr. White. "What can I do?" He rushes to the dishwasher, but it's already started. He checks the coffee pots, but they are upside down on the towels.

"Jimmy, it's all done. It's quitting time."

Jimmy is still haunted by Tim's words.

"Are you OK, Jimmy?"

"Yes, I'm fine, Mr. White." He grabs his coat from the back. "I'll see you Monday."

"Don't forget the treats!"

Jimmy backtracks to the kitchen to get the white cardboard box of muffins and shortbread that Mr. White has put aside for him. "Thank you," he says.

"Have a good weekend, Jimmy."

Jimmy leaves Main Street and turns onto Fifth Avenue. He makes a stop at the liquor store, then picks up a pizza. It's Friday. Everyone seems happier, proud of getting through the week and ready for some downtime. Jimmy was looking forward to the walk home, but now he barely notices it. Glen is sitting at the kitchen table, playing solitaire.

"What kind of treats do we have today?" he asks.

Jimmy passes him the box, cracks open a beer, and guzzles it.

"Hard day?" Glen asks.

"Sort of," he says.

"Well, sit down, have a game with me, unwind a bit," says Glenn.

"Nah, I'm going out," says Jimmy. He guzzles another beer and heads to the Tap.

Racing Thoughts

It's been two weeks since Jimmy saw Tim at the diner. His mind is bogged down with thought, tirelessly searching for answers to his questions. If what Tim said is true, then why hasn't Marley contacted him? If Tim hadn't come into The Family Diner, would Jimmy still be none the wiser?

Tim looked pleased to share news that wasn't his, hoping to watch Jimmy break. His tone judged Jimmy for something he knew nothing about. Marley knows where he lives. If she wants him to know she is having his child, why not tell him?

All the pieces float like shrapnel in his head. The slightest chance that it's true torments him day and night until he can't take it anymore. He makes several trips to the Tap, hoping to see Tim and call him on it, but there's been no sign of him or Marley.

He waits until Saturday night—Glen's dart night—to call Tim's bluff. He primes himself with a few drinks and dials Tim's number. It rings and rings. He's about to hang up when a woman answers.

"Is Tim around?" he asks.

"Tim is doing a night shift. Is there a message?"

"Who's this?" Jimmy asks.

"It's Roxy. Who's this?"

Jimmy doesn't answer. He should hang up. This is Tim's idea of a bad joke. "It's Jim Richards."

"Hi, Jimmy. I thought it was you. How are you? Tim says you have a job at the diner."

"I'm OK, I guess."

"Do you want me to tell Tim to give you a call?"

"No, that's OK. I mean, he's not too good at that, anyway. What he said to me at the diner—that was some kind of joke, right? Tim's way of messing with me?"

Roxy doesn't answer.

Jimmy remembers he's had one too many drinks and starts to go into a tailspin. "Never mind," he says. He shouldn't give that asshole the satisfaction of knowing he was duped. "I shouldn't have called."

"Wait, Jim," says Roxy. "It wasn't a lie. Marley is pregnant. It's yours, Jimmy."

Jimmy drops the receiver to his side as the words burn into his skull. He can still hear Roxy's voice in the distance.

"Jimmy, are you there? Hello?"

Jimmy puts the phone back to his ear but forgets to speak.

"Jimmy? Hello?"

"I'm still here," he says.

"Marley didn't want you to know. She says she wants to do this on her own. Tim had no business saying anything. She's just scared that you'll reject her. No one should raise a kid alone, Jimmy. You have a right to know. God, she's going to be pissed."

Jimmy feels sick. "I got to go." He hangs up the phone, staggers to his bedroom, and lies on his bed, trying to stop his head from spinning. He throws up on the floor and crashes back onto his bed, not sure if it's the beer or Roxy's words that want out. "It's yours" still ring in his ears.

The next morning, Jimmy wakes up to Glen's screaming. "Jim, answer the goddamn phone!"

Jimmy jumps to his feet, not sure if he's awake or in a dream.

"Who is it?"

"I don't fucking know, but it's been ringing all morning and it's for you."

Jimmy staggers into the door frame, bumping his arm and shoulder. His head feels like it's in a vise and his throat is parched. He grabs the phone in the living room, unsure if he will hear a voice on the other end of the line.

"Hello? Who is this?" he says.

"Glen sounds like a delight this morning."

"What?" says Jimmy. "Who is this?"

"It's Tim. Jimmy, are you awake?"

"Barely," he says.

"Well, wake up. I'm coming to get you in half an hour. Marley wants to talk."

A Commitment

The tension is heavy on the drive to Tim's house. Tim attempts to make small talk about the weather and the diner until Jimmy erupts.

"What the fuck is going on, Tim? If this is some kind of joke, then you are truly twisted. You've gone too far! What's all this bullshit about Marley?"

"Just hold up, Jim! Don't be mouthing off now. I know I shouldn't have told you the way I did, but it's just my way. Roxy and I are concerned about her. The girl is struggling, and she shouldn't have to do it on her own. Not when you're working, here in the same town. We thought you should know, but she made us swear not to tell. I saw you at the diner and I just couldn't keep it in. Anyway, she knows I told you and she agreed to see you. I'll drop you off at my house and give you a chance to talk."

Jimmy feels numb. He can barely keep himself off the street. What's he going to do with a baby? He doesn't speak for the rest of the drive. He doesn't know what to say, what to do. He has nothing.

Tim pulls up to the small house. Roxy comes out and opens the car door.

"Go ahead, Jimmy. Marley's inside," she says.

Jimmy watches the Bronco pull away and walks into the house.

Marley is curled up on the couch with the TV on.

"What's going on, Marley?" he says.

She turns off the TV and straightens up on the couch. She is a petite young woman, barely eighteen years old, with fair skin and blue eyes that look red from crying. She's wearing leggings and a baggy top. She puts out her cigarette and stares at Jimmy.

He's happy to see her pretty face.

"I don't know why you're here, Jimmy. I don't need you here. I haven't heard from you or seen you in months."

"Tim says you want to talk."

"What do you want to talk about, Jimmy?"

"Is it true?" he asks. "Are you having a baby?"

"Yes, it's true."

"Is it mine?"

"Well, I haven't been with anyone else."

"Why didn't you tell me?"

"Why should I tell you? You never called me. You didn't even say goodbye. I didn't think you would want to know."

"Well, I know now. I want to help. What do you want me to do? I have a good job. I mean, I don't make much money, but I get forty hours a week and I don't have to pay for gas or lunch. If it's mine, then I should help. Where are you living? We can do this together if you want. Every baby deserves to have parents."

"What do you know about being a parent?" she asks.

"About as much as you do, I guess. I know every little kid deserves a chance. They deserve more than I got, that's for sure. What do you say, Marley? Should we try this?" Jimmy is startled by his own words but figures they're the right ones to say. He has to do better than was done to him.

"I don't know, Jimmy. We can try," she says. "A baby deserves a chance."

Jimmy and Marley

They are an unusual couple. Physically, they couldn't look more different: Jimmy, a big, dark Indigenous boy, and Marley, petite and white as snow. But there is something else. They are as awkward as newborn fawns. Even at the ages of eighteen and nineteen, they somehow seem younger. Tim often remarks that seeing them together is like watching a couple of kids playing house. They meet life's challenges like head-on collisions, without the benefit of the learning that comes from such encounters. Their lack of wisdom dictates a tiring path. They raise more than one eyebrow out in the world, but neither of them seem to notice. They are too busy just getting through it.

Marley has a small apartment a few blocks down from Tim and Roxy. Jimmy moves in to combine his income from the diner with Marley's social assistance.

Roxy and Tim are their only real friends. Marley showed up on the west coast after she ran away from her Ontario home at the age of seventeen. Her father died and her mother's new husband was more interested in Marley than his new wife. After months of fighting him off, she finally found the courage to tell her mother what was happening, only to be accused of being jealous and sabotaging her mother's marriage.

She met Roxy at a shelter in Calgary and together, they decided to make their way to the northern British Columbia coast to plant trees and be near the ocean. They almost made it, until Roxy met up with Tim and Marley started growing a baby.

Despite the unexpected and abrupt start, Jimmy and Marley commit to their unborn baby and a dream of a better life. Jimmy talks to her about owning his own diner. He can already make most of Mr. White's recipes and has ideas of his own, like adding bannock bread and fish fry to the menu.

Marley quits smoking and Jimmy spends less time at the Tap. Things are going as well as can be expected, until Jimmy notices Marley's restless unease. She spends more time sleeping and always has a cold. He becomes really concerned when she stops going to her doctor's appointments. She tells him it's just her body trying to keep up with the growing a little human. Jimmy wants to believe her, but when he casually mentions it to Roxy, he detects something in her reaction, something she's not saying. He convinces Roxy to check in on Marley and leaves it at that.

A Secret

Marley waits until she hears Jimmy leave for work before she gets dressed and heads out. If she takes the nine o'clock bus, she can get back in plenty of time to cook supper. She knows the downtown area fairly well from the day trips she made with Roxy when they first arrived.

She spots Pink's Pharmacy in the distance and pulls the cord to exit. Hill View Apartments are close by, and she should have no trouble finding what she's looking for. She goes into Pink's and gets herself a tin of ginger ale and a straw. She takes a walk past the apartments until she's approached by one of the local businessmen riding a green bike.

He slows down and gives her his sales pitch. "Hey girl what are you looking for this morning? You need to chill?" She makes eye contact and nods. He stops. "You wanting some H?"

Marley nods.

"Twenty," he says.

Marley hands him the money.

"All right, girl," he says. He hauls a baggie of powder out of his pocket, hands it to her, and continues down the street, already focused on his next customer.

Marley finds a place in the park and spends most of the morning and early afternoon burning and inhaling the heroin. She feels mellow. Soft. Everything is beautiful again. No more edges.

She always tells herself one more time won't hurt. It's not like she's injecting it. No one will know.

She notices a familiar couple, Nikki and Calvin, approaching her. They are a permanent fixture in the area and live in a tent at the park. They are wobbly on their feet and crash down onto the grass next to her.

"When's the baby due?" asks Nikki. She reaches out and touches Marley's belly with her dirty hand. Marley pushes her hand away.

"Sorry," says Nikki. "You're an uptight one."

Calvin smiles at Marley. He hasn't showered in weeks and is missing several teeth. He takes a sip from his can of beer, then covers it with his coat.

"You scared her, doll. Take it easy, now. I'm sure the baby will have the face of an angel, like its mama," he says.

"I'm just twenty-four weeks," says Marley.

They sit together and Nikki passes around a joint. Calvin clenches his jaw and twitches when he speaks. "Hey, Marley, looks like you need a hit. You're too low now. You need to come back up."

He takes out a pipe and begins heating the bowl. Marley remembers seeing him before. Roxy said he looked like bad news.

Marley feels anxious. She's too buzzed. She gets to her feet.

"I have to go," she says.

"Wait!" says Calvin.

Marley rushes away as their voices laugh behind her. She makes her way out of the park in search of a bus stop, her feet barely touching the ground. She pats her belly and tells her baby it will be fine. She can't find a bus stop but sees a bus approaching and waves her arms frantically. To her surprise, it stops, and she climbs on. She digs in her pocket for change. She feels like she is moving in slow motion. She looks at the coins but is unable to focus. She drops a handful of them into the metal container.

"Can you stop when we get to King's Corner Store, please? Thank you, sir, for stopping. I really appreciate it."

"You were at a bus stop, kid. That's how this works," he says.

Marley laughs. Everyone seems to be staring at her. She wipes her nose and looks for a seat, staggering to the back of the bus. She lays her head against the window, trying to make sense of where she is. She yells from her seat, "King's Corner Store!" The bus driver glares at her in the rear-view mirror.

The woman across from her is looking at her belly and shaking her head. Marley wants to cry but refuses to give in. *She has no right to judge. She doesn't know me. She doesn't know what it's like. She probably has a family and people to help her. She can go to hell.*

Marley makes it home and rushes to the bathroom. Her bladder is bursting. She washes her hands and pauses in the mirror. It's going to be OK, she tells herself. She reapplies her makeup and changes her clothes. She changes three times until she finds what she wants.

She remembers supper and rushes to the kitchen to turn on the oven. She takes some frozen patties and buns out of the freezer, oils a pan, and turns on the stove. She decides her clothes are too tight for her growing belly and goes back to the bedroom to change again. The voice in her head tells her she looks high. She goes back to the mirror and brushes her hair.

"What are you doing?" says the voice. "Nobody wants you. This baby won't love you. You don't deserve it."

She is pulled out of her head by Roxy's voice at her front door.

Marley decides not to answer the door and continues looking in her closet. Suddenly, the voice sounds closer.

"Marley, are you in here?"

"Yes, I'm here," she says. She lights a cigarette.

"Why didn't you answer the door?"

"I was in the bathroom," she says.

"I thought you quit smoking."

"I did, but I slipped today. I will quit again tomorrow." Marley avoids eye contact and puts out her cigarette.

"I brought you some clothes for the baby," Roxy says. "We found some good deals at the garage sale. Hardly used."

"Oh, that's great!" says Marley. She reaches for the miniature sleeper.

Roxy is staring at Marley's face. "Are you high?" she asks.

"What? No. What are you talking about?"

"Oh, God. You're slurring. Marley, Jimmy's going to know. He already suspects there's something up."

"It's just one time, Rox. I was so wired. I needed it."

"You needed it! You're back to that, are you? I'm sure that baby doesn't need it."

"It's just once, Rox. The baby is fine. She's happy when I'm happy."

"Jimmy's going to know, Marley."

"Jimmy don't know shit," she says.

"What's that smell? Are you burning something?"

"I'm making supper."

"You mean you're burning supper!" Roxy runs to the kitchen, takes the smoking pan off the stove, and opens a window. She looks at her watch. "Go take a shower. I'll cook the burgers."

"I don't need a shower," says Marley.

Roxy stops what she's doing and takes Marley's hands. "Marley, what are you doing with that heavy makeup on? You look like one of the hookers downtown. Go take a shower and snap out of this before Jimmy gets home."

Marley gets in the shower while Roxy oils another pan. After an hour, Roxy looks for Marley in her bedroom.

"You look a little better," she says. "Marley maybe you should talk to someone. You can't do this again. Jimmy is playing it straight, cutting down his drinking, working every day. He won't want this."

"It was just one slip, Rox, that's it." Marley lights another cigarette.

"I'm not stupid, Marley. It wasn't just once. Jimmy's been asking me why you're so tired and sniffling all the time. I can take you to the clinic. I'll help you through this. Please think about it, Marley." Roxy gives her a hug and leaves.

Jimmy's an hour late getting home. He carries two bags of groceries and a can of ginger ale for Marley. He's relieved to see her up and feeling better. He pretends not to notice the smell of cigarette smoke. The ashtray is clean. He praises her for the tasty burgers and helps with the dishes. They sit on the couch, and he rubs her belly.

"Have you thought of any names yet?" he asks.

"Not really," she says. Marley notices the scars on Jimmy's hand and rubs them with her fingers. "What happened here?"

"I burnt it when I was small. I was too close to a fire," he says. "There's nothing to tell, just a stupid accident."

"Where were your parents?" she asks.

Jimmy ignores the question. "How about Robin? It would work for a boy or girl. It was my brother's name. We called him Robbie."

"What happened to him?" she asks.

"We were separated in the foster system."

"Do you know where he is?"

"No. I'm not sure. I haven't seen him in a long time."

Marley is reminded how little she and Jimmy really know about each other. He avoids most of her questions and never talks about his family, but he doesn't press her about hers, either. They both seem to be running from something.

This baby will have no cousins or grandparents, no roots or stories from the past. It will be just the three of them. It makes her feel lonely. She convinces herself it's probably for the best this way. The fewer people in this baby's life, the lower the chances of disappointment.

"I like Robin," she says. She's glad Roxy saved dinner and the evening. She decides to take the bus to the clinic in the morning. She'll get the early bus, at eight a.m., so she's home early.

The Last Time

The next morning, Marley leaves the apartment with Jimmy, and when he turns to go up Main Street, she stays at the corner bus stop. He kisses her goodbye.

"Good luck. I'll see you tonight," he says.

The bus is on time and she finds a place in the back. It's only four or five blocks to the clinic. She watches out the window and can see it in the distance. Thankfully, there are only a few cars. The wait time should be short. Jimmy will be eager to hear the report. She will tell the nurses she was feeling too sick to come last time but that she's having a good day today.

She reaches for the cord, but stops herself. She watches as the bus passes the blue building. It's early. She has plenty of time. She'll get out on the way back.

She takes the bus all the way downtown and tells herself this is the last time.

When Jimmy returns home, he finds Roxy and Tim in his living room.

"I didn't know you guys were coming," he says. "Where's Marley? What did the doctor say?"

"Jim," says Tim, standing.

Jimmy sings out to Marley, "Marley, come on out."

He looks in the kitchen. She didn't start supper today. Then he notices Tim standing.

"What's wrong?" he asks. "Did she get bad news?"

Roxy speaks. "Jimmy, just sit down for a minute. We need to talk to you."

Jimmy sits. So does Tim. Jimmy can sense there is something wrong. "Is it the baby? Where's Marley?"

"Jimmy, there's something Marley wasn't telling you."

Jimmy remains silent. She left him. The baby wasn't his after all.

Tim speaks. "Jimmy, Marley was a user."

Jimmy looks confused. "What do you mean, user?"

"Heroin. She used heroin, Jimmy. She tried hard to stop for the baby and for you, but she couldn't. It had a bad hold on her."

"What do you mean she tried hard? Where is she now?"

Roxy starts to cry.

"Jimmy, she overdosed. I'm so sorry. She didn't make it," says Tim.

Jimmy jumps up from the couch. He silently walks away from them, grasping at his hair as if he needs something to hold on to. He feels like he can't breathe. He bends over and tries to catch his breath. Tim jumps up and tries to get him to sit. Jimmy backs away from Tim.

"What about the baby? Where's the baby?" Jimmy asks.

Tim looks at Roxy for help. "Jimmy, I'm so sorry. The baby was too small to survive."

All the colour drains from Jimmy's face. He feels numb, empty. His head begins to spin. He feels like he is going to pass out. He holds on to the back of a chair and looks up at them.

"Where are they? I need to see them," he says.

"We will take you there," says Tim.

Saying Goodbye

When they arrive at Northern Health, Jimmy and Roxy are taken to a hospital room, where Marley is covered with a sheet. Jimmy sits next to her, uncovers her face, and holds her hand. He bows his head and speaks softly. He apologizes for all the things he didn't know and tells her he's sorry their time together was so short. He tells her she deserves peace, off the street and with people she can trust, and he forgives her for leaving him.

The nurse asks him if he wants to hold his baby. He takes the small bundle in his arms and looks at his tiny son's face. He looks familiar. He kisses him on the head and sings to him. He walks around the room holding him close. He would have tried his very best to be a good father. He feels a wave of joy and sorrow, and then a crash of pain, like he's been chewed up and spit out. His life with Marley was a lie. If he had only known, he would have helped her! It was his baby too! His son. He feels stupid for having had a dream. He knows better. These things never work out. He doesn't get to have a better life. Not him, not now, not ever.

Three days before his twentieth birthday, Jimmy Richards buries his family at St. Mary Cemetery on the outskirts of the city. This stretch of land is surrounded by rugged, steep cliffs that watch over the untethered souls, their life stories etched in stone on the ground below. An eagle glides overhead, witnessing this addition: *Marley Duval and Robin Duval Richards. Mother and son forever in our hearts*. Their short lives are marked by two white crosses in a sea of lives once lived.

Roxy, Tim, and a local priest join him for a quiet ceremony. Jimmy lays a single red rose at the base of each cross. The eagle cries out above. Jimmy looks to the sky, silently cursing his life and the missing relatives he's never known. He resents the rites of passage he was never shown, and the lessons never learned.

He pushes it all down, hardens his shell, and thanks the priest, Tim, and Roxy for coming.

Roxy hugs him. "Jimmy, come back with us for a couple of days. We'll cook you a good meal. We can have a drink."

He doesn't look at her. He's too numb for kindness. He walks away from the gravesite.

"Jimmy, at least let us give you a ride!" Tim shouts.

Jimmy doesn't look back. Without a word to anyone, he leaves Fort Marin for good.

A War in the Woods

Mary Marcel hasn't been much good for anything after her walk with Jonah in the forest. They agreed it was important to see the reported massacre with their own eyes. Tribal elders had warned them that the government had given away the valley and a clear-cutting was planned.

Jonah now wonders if it was a good idea to take Mary there. Neither of them was prepared to see the massive veterans haphazardly strewn across the ground, nor the earth heaved up to release the giant cedars and firs from their strong roots. They had been tethered there for hundreds of years but their longevity meant nothing to the butchers. Not even Big Red was spared. How anyone could carry out such mass destruction without a moment's hesitation was beyond Mary's nature to imagine.

Jonah had seen it before. He learned to expect disrespect and his heart could carry the weight. But through Mary's eyes, it was violence.

"A barbaric assault," she called it.

Jonah believed she could feel the earth screaming with horror, and that was why it hit her so hard, why she grieved. She imagined her ancestors before her felt the same when they were invaded. How their connection to the land, the rivers, and the animals were severed in the same thoughtless way.

"It has never really stopped," she said. "And now this."

She paced for hours after their return, mumbling and ranting until exhaustion forced sleep. Jonah consoled her as best he could, keeping his fishing days short and preparing food that comforted her. Her children visited, sang songs, made jokes, and received a few fleeting smiles, but her spirit was hard to revive.

In desperation, they reached out to Jonathan, who had a special connection with his foster mother. He shared her love of the old growth and was inspired to fight for them at every opportunity. When Lisa called to tell him Mary, Jonah, and the Nuu-chah-nulth elders needed them, it didn't take any convincing for him to push back his agenda and catch the earliest flight home.

The years spent with the Nuu-chah-nulth Nation were a rebirth for Jonathan and Lisa. The Marcels embraced them like they were family from day one. They were loved as if they had been born right there under their tiny cedar roof. They learned to love nature and slowly began to feel like they belonged to something bigger than themselves. Jonathan's pain healed and his life was filled with a renewed energy of gratitude that was always with him. It became a living force behind everything he pursued.

Life in Conuma not only saved him, but prepared him for something greater: an opportunity to share what had been given to him. Hope for a better life. He owed his family everything.

After law school, Jonathan discovered his special niche was fighting for the underdog. A tendency he often joked he was destined to fulfill. He found himself with endless opportunities to put his teachings to the test, both in and out of the courtroom. His dogged determination earned him a formidable reputation in legal circles. Activists and last-chance victims admired his candor and willingness to fight injustice. But those who preferred to keep the applecart in good working order, he drew disdain—a fact that bore no weight on his conscience.

Early in his career, he met a kindred spirit in Bethany Leslie, a Black activist who was building a career defending human rights internationally. Jonathan found himself consulting with her on matters of racial profiling and child welfare violations on a regular basis. The two worked closely on several high-profile human rights cases and developed a deep love and respect for one another. While their demanding career paths meant they had limited time together, they agreed life was better together and, somehow, they made it work. Bethany was torn that she couldn't join Jonathan and his family, but a high-stakes case prevented her from leaving. She knew they were in good hands and Jonathan left with her blessing.

Now, the sacred lands of his ancestors are at risk once again. The Nuu-chah-nulth have been stewards of the lands around Clayoquot Sound for generations. They are shocked at the industrial-scale forestry being practiced and the complete lack of consultation around land-use planning in their territories.

The stakes are very high. The government of British Columbia sold off sixty-five percent of Crown land to the highest bidder, giving the biggest logging company a pass to clear cut massive old-growth trees all the way down to the rich valley bottom and allowing them free rein of the valley's intricate ecosystem. Such a comprehensive swipe will assuredly devastate salmon streams and animal habitats for generations to come, all while removing a vital carbon sink for the entire planet.

Word is out and communities from all over the valley are divided. Some see the project as necessary for job growth, and a cash injection for local families. Others see it as short-sighted and blatant disrespect for old growth and natural habitats, and a shocking disregard for preservation practices. Indigenous council chiefs, community members, environmentalists, and even celebrities south of the border have gathered in an act of public but peaceful disobedience to protect the area. They met at dawn at a local bridge junction where logging trucks entered to clear cut the area, including significant stands of old-growth forest.

Thousands of people have joined their cause. Dozens sit in the middle of the street, singing peacefully as they block the giant trucks from passing through. Others stand together, arms and hands intertwined, forming a human fence in defense of the voiceless forest behind them. Jonathan witnesses the colour rush back to Mary's cheeks as she sings songs of protection for the forest.

Mary tells Jonathan that cutting the limbs of the cedars is like cutting her own limbs, and watching them fall feels as though her own feet have been taken out from under her. She has to give the land a voice.

Jonathan and Jonah take their turn sitting in the street to stop the massive trucks from passing through. Jonathan senses that the police are coming for them. He quickly turns to Jonah.

"Let your body go completely limp, Jonah. Don't resist. Let them do their work. It's going to be OK. Be like the jelly fish!" He's barely said his words when two large police officers grab him by the feet and shoulders. Jonathan smiles peacefully as he is forced into the police van with the others. Jonah lands behind him with a thud.

"Hey," shouts Jonathan. "That was unnecessary. He's an elder!"

"It's OK, Jonathan. I'm OK," Jonah says.

Jonah pushes himself to his feet and takes his place on the bench across from his son.

"They aren't playing fair. We aren't offering any resistance!" Jonathan shouts at the slamming door.

"Did you really think they would?" Jonah asks.

Jonathan bows his head, smiling. "That's my problem. I have too much damn hope."

As the van pulls out, a dozen other protestors take their places in the street. Supporters line the roads to bear witness to the massive response, assuring the demonstrations remain peaceful.

They chant in unison: "You can't arrest us all!"

They shout and tap on the van in support of their detained allies. The frustrated loggers rev their engines and threaten to charge the blockade, hurling their own sentiments from the safety of their trucks.

"Welfare bums, go home!"

Jonathan and Jonah's night in the crowded cell is an unusual and new experience for them both.

"Well, Jonah look at it this way. Daiji would say this night will deepen our understanding of peaceful protest and speed up our healing and progress." He winks at Jonah.

"I'm an old man, Jonathan. How many ways must I learn? Besides, I thought lawyers are supposed to keep you out of jail, not put you in! You might have to give back that grant money," says Jonah.

"You may be right," Jonathan says with a laugh.

Jonah continues his lament. "Now we're going to miss out on Mary's moose stew and berry pie."

Father and son laugh and remain upbeat despite their growling bellies. They are released the next day, thanks to a growing number of cell mates, and quickly rejoin their family, who continue the effort by feeding the supporters.

Though the logging and protests continue for months, the resistance pays off. The arrests of youth, elders, and environmentalists across all cultures are seen on television screens and in newspapers around the world, forcing the logging company and the government to the table. Within the next two years, the largest logging company in the province loses at least two hundred million in pulp, paper, and wood contracts and, in an unexpected irony, sells its rights to First Nations communities. The standoff becomes just one of many future battles to protect the land.

Jonathan returns to the city, energized by the belief that if enough minds and souls protect what's important to the majority, a point is reached when their vision becomes reality.

Jonathan's life has purpose. They must continue to push.

A Purpose

A grizzly bear takes slow, laboured steps across the hot, black earth, searching for a reprieve from the scorching air and noxious heat. With her cub at her side, she raises her head to the dense, yellow sky, begging for a cool breath. But none is found. No garbage bin, shallow stream, or cache in sight. It's a miracle they've survived at all, as most have not. Her fur is visibly singed, leaving coarse grey and black marks across her back, and her ear is dripping blood. The cub at her side struggles with burnt paws as he obeys his mother's cues to keep moving.

Bush pilot Paul Turner is flying low, making a final scan for survivors and salvageable fire equipment. He calls the bear sighting into wildlife, much to the shock of the responder.

"That's a bloody miracle. I'll get someone out there as soon as I can. How big is she?"

"She's a four hundred pounder for sure. A mama with a cub."

"OK, roger that."

"Can you take us down?" Jay Michaels is a photographer who hitched a ride in the forestry chopper to capture the devastation of the biggest wildfire that has ever engulfed the island. "I have to get this scene. It's total annihilation and she's having the fight of her life."

"Will do," says Paul.

Jay knows he will be paid well for the photos but that's not his motive. People need to see the devastation and silent victims of what he considers over-consumption and human greed. He works for *Science Today* and has been documenting the signs of climate change for years. Over two decades into the twenty first century and every person over the age of ten has heard the warnings. Society has lost its appetite for denial. "How far out is wildlife rescue?" Jay asks.

"Won't take them long. They have a crew just outside town."

"What about water? Can I leave them a jug"?

"What, for the bears?"

"Yeah, there's nothing down there for them. I'm surprised they're still walking."

"Yeah, man, whatever, but you do know that's a grizzly, right?"

"Yeah, yeah, I won't get close. I'll leave it where she can see it. The blades will keep her back."

Jay jumps out of the chopper, finds a place just outside the heli-squall. He zooms in on the majestic bear, who is scorched and staggering with her cub. He takes all the pictures he needs then retrieves a knife from his pack. He quickly cuts the tops off two large jugs of water, wasting as little of the precious contents as possible. He leaves it ten meters out, directly in her path, and runs back to the chopper.

Within seconds, they're lifting back into the sky. The smoke is thick from hectares of fire and gas. The air is barely breathable. Jay coughs as the particulates reach deep inside his lungs.

"It's hard to breathe down there," he says. "How did they ever make it? There's nothing left."

"She's going for it!" Paul reports.

Jay takes another shot of the small cub drinking from his makeshift well.

"Hang in there, little fella," he says.

"The wildlife crew are pretty keen to save what they can. They'll make it," says Paul.

"Yeah, but will the rest of us?" says Jay.

A New Reality

Fire continues to rage down the eastern coast of the island. It's day twenty-five. Thirty thousand hectares have burned. Entire communities have been devastated. Hundreds of buildings and homes have been lost.

The severe fire rating and incessant high winds have made suppression impossible. First responders from all over the country have joined high-risk crews in a relentless battle against active fires, while the majority of resources have been shifted to prevention measures in order to contain the rest of the island. It will take a monumental effort, as the reported firestorms are so large and hot that they have generated their own unpredictable and extremely dangerous weather systems.

Recovery crews on the western side of the island are attending to all displaced life forms, both two- and four-legged. Sites have been set up to provide temporary relief until secondary housing arrangements are in place.

The scene has the look and feel of a refugee camp. With blank faces, survivors wander the grounds in the oppressive heat, searching for water, a blanket, or the nearest toilet. A teenage girl is crying and frantically working her phone in search of friends and family.

"Mom, where are you?" she says. "Is everyone OK? Our house is gone!"

A bearded man in work clothes and a safety vest shouts at one of the workers about how things should have been different.

"We could have saved our homes! We were evacuated too soon! The responders were too late."

The crisis contingency plan is in high gear. Schools and community centres are full and services spill onto the streets. Any open space will do. A collection of tents serves as clinics, kitchens, shelters, and information centres. Health care workers triage as best they can. They clean and bandage the wounded and rehydrate the exhausted while air ambulances transport the severely injured to the designated hospital. Business and community groups have responded in full force, rolling out a hodgepodge of donated meals. Volunteers find the mentally wounded a place to lie down.

Lisa Watson takes her place on the ground, multitasking among them all. She works the registration table, taking the names and numbers of those who have lost their homes, and directs them to the temporary accommodation area. Most will be transported to Vancouver, where hotels have been transformed into shelters until relocations can be worked out. The western perimeter of the island is safe for now, but survivors continue to arrive daily.

Lisa is taking a break from her brother's campaign to help at the fire camps. Jonathan, too, has been working nonstop, with little sleep for days. The number of human fatalities has reached the double digits, and animals have perished by the hundreds. He is filled with grief for the families who have lost everything and the hundreds of plant, animal, and insect species that have disappeared in the flaming forest. The destruction of biodiversity at this scale will have unimaginable impacts on human life.

Despite the full panel of emotions he's feeling, it's the anger and frustration that are difficult to manage. Scientists have been warning that longer and more frequent periods of extreme high temperatures will have major repercussions. The large, resilient old-growth forests retain moisture and help regulate the climate, but today they have all but disappeared due to an increase in logging and politicians with pockets stuffed full of money.

Bigger, hotter fires increase the carbon and gas emissions in the atmosphere, speeding up global warming and producing more mega-fires with astounding reoccurrence. The earth has been bled dry and science has been ignored.

Jonathan overhears Lisa's desperate attempt to troubleshoot yet another disturbing situation to the site manager.

"We need a way to fast track the seniors. They are confused and vulnerable. We have to get them off this island ASAP."

"I agree," says Linda Fisk, the service manager.

"What if we try to connect them with support in Vancouver and send them straight to the outgoing accommodation area? We'll skip all the non-urgent assessments here and save that for the city."

"OK," says Lisa. "I'll set up a new station for seniors only."

"I'll let the others know what we're doing," says Linda.

"Hey, it's time for a break," says Jonathan. "Let's go to the cafeteria for dinner. There's someone I want you to meet."

Jonathan and Lisa make their way to the food tent, where lines of volunteers churn out sustenance on heated serving trays in an attempt to soothe and comfort. A young Australian man joins them at their table.

"Lisa, this is Jay," says Jonathan. "He works at *Science Today*. He has been working for me on the campaign from Vancouver. He helped get all our websites and Twitter feeds up and running. He has been traveling with Forest Services and getting photos of the destruction. I asked him to share some with us so we can start our campaign on the environmental impacts."

"Hello, it's a pleasure to meet you, Lisa," Jay says. "Jonathan has told me a lot about you."

"I have heard of your work as well. What did you get today?"

Jay opens his laptop and shares his three hundred shots of the day. They solemnly review the destruction and mayhem captured in the slideshow.

"It feels like I'm watching a funeral," says Jonathan.

"We are," says Lisa.

Jay breaks the melancholy. "You need a success story? Look at her." He scrolls to the end of the roll to show them the mother grizzly and her cub, surrounded by the smoking, charred earth. "I think this should be the cover photo."

"That's an amazing photo," says Lisa. "Are they OK?"

"Yes, wildlife officers picked them up and are releasing them somewhere more hospitable."

"Great work," says Jonathan.

"Thank you. But I'm just taking a few snaps. You guys are in the trenches, doing the real work. How are people holding up?"

"As well as can be expected," responds Jonathan. "Considering life as they've known it is changing abruptly."

"Where are you headed tomorrow?" asks Lisa.

"I'm traveling up north, where another fire has gained momentum. They're trying to save Blackwater the oil and gas site."

"Really?" says Jonathan. "I hadn't heard."

"Paul and I just got wind of it as we were checking in with the incident commander."

"Why there?" asks Lisa.

"I like to get all sides of the picture, for the full story," responds Jay.

"Excuse me while I garner up some sympathy," says Lisa.

"I hear you," says Jay. "But the truth of the matter is that we are all in this together now. We don't have time to pick sides."

Lisa gives him a reluctant nod and stands, taking her tray. "Well, if you'll excuse me, I have to check on Mrs. Dixon. She lost her home and her husband is on shaky ground."

"OK, I will check in with you later," says Jonathan.

"OK, bro." Lisa heads to Tent Four.

"Yikes," says Jay. "I didn't mean to . . ."

"Don't worry about it. She's exhausted and frustrated like the rest of us."

"Jonathan, I would like you to come with me tomorrow," says Jay. "It will be a different perspective for you. The workers running the station are as scared as the rest of us. They are tied to it because they make their living there. We are all just trying to survive."

"That's some crazy spin you have there, brother. What do you really want?"

"I would love to have you with me, mate," says Jay. "I can always use that unique lens you carry, and it will be easier to get permission from the incident commander if you're with me."

"Ah, there we go. You need special permission, do you? As long as that *unique lens* doesn't cause too much grief. They may not want a green humanitarian treading on their turf."

"Honestly, I think anyone in Blackwater who hasn't already evacuated will be preoccupied with saving their asses," says Jay.

"OK, Jay, you have me for a day. I'll try to get debriefed on it, but we shouldn't expect to make friends," says Jonathan.

"OK by me. I tend to keep to myself anyway," says Jay.

Unintended Consequences

Jonathan waits for Jay at the heli launchpad and stares at the grey sky. The low-pressure system and light winds will make their six-thirty start achievable; finally, a reprieve from the thick smoke.

Blackwater is almost two hundred kilometres northeast, and it will take a few hours of flying time to get there. The forestry service's tight flight restrictions mean their route won't be as the crow flies—another long day.

Jay's Wrangler pulls in, and he and Paul get out.

"You all set?" asks Jay.

"For better or for worse," says Jonathan.

"We have to check in with the incident commander before we take off. Come join us."

Jonathan joins Jay and Paul at forestry service headquarters. The small room has been a hub of intel and communications for weeks. Maps and computer screens are a burst of colour codes, giving intricate details of the massive terrain management plan. The red areas continue to expand where out of control fires are claiming more ground and suppression measures have stopped. The hopeful yellow pins represent the areas crews are trying to save, and the black slowly transforms the map like a creeping plague, indicating scorched earth.

The calm demeanour of the incident commander, Martin Rhodes, seems incongruous with the task at hand. He checks weather radars, directs ground and air crews, and makes calculated decisions based on unpredictable conditions. His assistants have a constant eye on the wind, weather, maps, and available crew.

Jay helps himself to the coffee and pours Jonathan a cup.

Paul checks in with Rhodes. "How's it looking, Marty? Any chance we'll get up in the next hour?"

"I think so, Paul. The low pressure is taking hold, giving us a breather from the smoke. Visibility is the best it's been in days, but it's busy out there." He looks at Jay and Jonathan. "I was told you had a special guest this morning. Hello, Mr. Richards. How are you?"

Jonathan shakes Rhodes's hand. "Not special, just concerned like you. Thank you for the wonderful and extremely difficult job you are doing for us."

"We're doing what we can," says Rhodes. "It's far from over, I'm afraid."

"What does the northeast look like? Is it possible to get out this morning?"

"Well, most of the crews have moved west, so it's not as busy as it was, but it's starting to pick up again. The compressor station is at risk, and we're sending a crew to check it out. The company has their own crew, so shouldn't be too much traffic. Here's the NOTAM. Make yourself familiar."

"NOTAM?" Jonathan asks.

"Notice to airmen," Rhodes says. "You need to stay five nautical miles outside of our fire perimeter and keep our channels clear."

"Yes, sir. Will do," says Paul.

"Where are you headed, exactly?" asks Rhodes.

"Blackwater."

"Blackwater! You'll have to keep it tight. Like I said, there's new burning there. Stay away from the site! If those chemicals go up, it's bad news."

"Will do, chief," says Paul.

Paul, Jay, and Jonathan head to the launchpad and board the chopper.

"Jonathan, everyone has been evacuated. Are you sure you want to do this?" asks Paul.

"We'll play it straight," says Jonathan. "Follow the NOTAM. If we don't get there, we don't get there. We can't put anyone at risk. Emergency crews are busy enough without having to worry about us."

"Roger that," says Paul.

"Jay, what kind of images are you hoping to get?" asks Jonathan.

"I'll know when I see it," Jay says.

"A response to the unanticipated, I suspect."

"Unintended consequences of oil and gas? Who would have thought?" says Jonathan.

"Unintended consequences of being human," says Jay.

Jonathan gives a sad nod. The noise in his head is as loud as the chopper blades. Yes, progress—this is where it has gotten the world.

Five kilometres out, Paul notices an unusual movement below.

"What the hell? Do you see that?"

"It looks like a herd of elk?" says Jay.

"No, they's caribou," says Jonathan. "What are they doing?"

"Trying to get the hell out of there," says Paul.

"Look at the slope they're on! They're too high up, too close to the fire and smoke," says Jay.

"That is odd," says Jonathan. "There must be a reason. Are we close to the Blackwater site?"

"Yes, it's just ahead," says Paul. He points at the hazy horizon.

"That's why. There's nowhere else to go. When the site was built, the animals were forced into the higher terrain because their habitats were replaced by roads and infrastructure. The animals are caught in the middle," says Jonathan.

"You're right," says Jay. "The fire has pushed them down, but they don't seem to want to go any lower."

"They have been pushed into a very slim corridor," says Jonathan.

The three men are silenced by their bird's-eye view of the herd attempting to traverse a steep slope.

"Look, some of them have fallen," says Jay.

"They're probably exhausted," says Jonathan.

Paul manages to bring the chopper a little closer for Jay to capture the unusual scene.

"Can we land nearby? I'd like to get a closer look," says Jay.

"I don't know," says Paul. "Do you see any breaks?"

"There!" says Jonathan. "To the left, above the slope, there's a ridge. Is that a clearing? Let's check it out."

Paul makes a couple of passes and finds a clearing big enough to land in. "OK, this will work." He carefully hovers the craft onto the most level patch of terrain he can find. "Do you have masks?" he asks.

"Yes," Jonathan secures a mask on his face and hands one to Jay.

"You don't have much time. We didn't account for this stop, so we have to watch our fuel," says Paul.

Jonathan and Jay make their way through the clearing, heading away from the chopper. Jonathan stops and begins looking around. Jay stops, too.

"Do you hear that?" asks Jonathan.

"It's the birds. What are they doing?" asks Jay. "There's so many of them."

The two men look around the forest. The birds are swooping, chirping, and hopping from tree to tree, but not gracefully or purposefully. They're frenzied, out of sync.

"Maybe no more than usual, but they are all chirping at once! They're panicked."

Jonathan and Jay try to take in the unusual activity of the birds.

"They sense the danger. It's pretty obvious," Jonathan says.

"Look, there!" Jay points to Jonathan's right.

The caribou are just below the ridge they're standing on. Jay gets his camera out and begins shooting the horrific exodus.

"Do you smell that?" asks Jonathan. "No wonder they won't go any lower."

"It must be from the compressor station. Here, have a look." Jay passes Jonathan his camera.

Jonathan scans the procession of frantic animals running along the steep corridor. His heart sinks. He can almost see the panic in their eyes as they try to escape the smoke above them and the ominous smell and danger below. He takes a few more photos. The sound of pounding hooves and snapping branches vibrates panic into his chest. He wonders what their collective instinct is telling them. Do they have a destination in mind, or are they just desperately fleeing?

"This feels ominous," says Jonathan.

"Nature in distress is a disturbing sight," says Jay.

"We shouldn't be here, Jay. It's not safe."

"OK, let's go," says Jay.

They quickly make their way back to the chopper.

"Was it as bad as it looks?" asks Paul.

"Worse," says Jonathan, trying to catch his breath.

"I have what I need," says Jay. "Let's try to make it to the site."

"It's sounding pretty hectic down there," says Paul.

The radio is busy with crew directives, updates, and warnings.

"We have to move out."

"It's out of control. We are moving out," says a crew member on the ground.

Paul points to a plume of black smoke on the horizon. "That would be it," he says. "We have to move further out. It sounds like the fire's perimeter has expanded."

As the chopper gets closer, a shocking visual comes into focus.

The fire has somehow crossed the site's many buffer zones and firewalls, and has ignited the infrastructure that houses a multitude of toxic substances. The company's emergency protocol has been stymied.

"This is devastating," says Jonathan.

"Looks like they couldn't get a grip on it at all," says Paul. "Thankfully the community has already been evacuated."

"The NG Group said their own fire protocols were designed to handle forest fire encroachment," says Jonathan.

"Well, this doesn't look handled to me," says Jay. "Do we have time for one last stop?"

"I can't get close to that," says Paul. "I can get you half a kilometre west, just outside the perimeter. You'll have to hoof it the rest of the way. Be quick—we need to avoid that black smoke or we'll have no visibility. Fifteen minutes tops. Keep your phones close."

Jonathan takes the emergency pack, pulling out two N95 masks. "This is the best that I have."

"OK," says Jay.

They put on the masks and Jonathan secures the pack. They jump out of the helicopter and quickly move toward the site.

The sky is an ominous grey, and the once-fresh forest air is replaced with a thick grey blanket of choking gas and smoke. The toxic clouds rain a fine ash that coats the nose, throat, and lungs. Jonathan watches as it quietly lands on his clothes. "It actually looks like it's snowing," he says.

"Yeah," says Jay. "But it's missing that nostalgic feeling."

The smell of gas and chemicals sends chills down Jonathan's spine. Emergency sirens are bellowing from the site. It sounds like a war zone.

"We're upwind," says Jay. "We should be able to get within two or three hundred metres. I can get a good shot from that distance. We won't go any closer."

The station comes into sight. The two men stand in silence.

"Wow, unbelievable," Jay gasps.

"They couldn't stop it," says Jonathan.

The compressor station and a holding tank are on fire. The crews have all pulled back. Jay drops his bag and takes pictures from every angle.

"That's it," he says. "We're done. We can't get any closer. It's too dangerous."

"OK, let's go," says Jonathan. "While we still can."

Jonathan is about to speak into the radio and tell Paul they are returning when they hear a woman's voice.

A firefighter and a woman limp out of the smoke toward them.

"We need help." The woman is helping the older man walk. Her blue eyes peer out from her ash-covered face, and the mask over her mouth and nose is coated in black soot. "My father is hurt. He burned his arms and is having difficulty breathing."

"What happened?" asks Jay.

Jonathan pulls the first aid pack off his back. The woman shouts over the siren. "They were trying to stop the fire from spreading but things got out of control! My father got trapped there!" She coughs.

Jonathan opens the first aid kit and takes out the saline and sterile gauze. "This is all I have!" He quickly bandages the man's forearms, then opens a bottle of water and manages to pour a little into his throat.

"Where's the rest of the crew?" asks Jay.

"There is no crew. They had to pull out and establish a new perimeter, but my foolish father thought he could do this on his own."

"Is he with the forestry service?" asks Jonathan.

"No, he's with the company."

Jay and Jonathan share a confused look.

"Let's get him to the chopper," says Jay. "Maybe we can touch down at the nearest hospital." Jay speaks into the radio, letting Paul know what's happening.

"OK, let's do it. It's going to be tight. We can't lose the daylight," Paul fires back.

Jay and Jonathan get the old man to his feet and help him back to the chopper. "I know this hurts, but it's short-lived. You have to push through it."

The old man groans loudly as the two men pull him into the helicopter.

"Is he going to be OK?" asks Paul.

"I don't know," says Jay. "Can we get him to Chelsey General?"

"Yes, but we'll have to stop at the airport to refuel if we're going to make it back."

"Let's do it," says Jonathan.

"I think we have time. We still have a few more hours of daylight. We'll get there," says Paul.

Jonathan hands the woman a spare set of headphones. She tearfully thanks the three men for their help. "Everyone else pulled out. If I didn't come looking for him, he would have been left behind. His name is Douglas. I am his daughter, Ashley." Her voice is hoarse.

"I'm glad we could help," says Jay.

Paul informs air control of the emergency request while Jay alerts the hospital. Jonathan attempts to comfort the young woman, who is coughing and clearly exhausted.

"I'm Jonathan. This is Jay and Paul."

"I can't thank you enough," she says. "I didn't think we were going to make it."

"You will both need medical attention. You may have breathed in some dangerous chemicals."

She nods. "Yes."

Jonathan looks at Douglas, who is lying on the back seat, and hands Ashley some ibuprofen. "It might help him a little," he says.

Douglas is flat on his back with his eyes closed. Ashley lifts her father's head and gives him the pills with some water. "You are going to be OK, Dad. We're on our way to the hospital."

Douglas nods slightly, his eyes still closed.

Ashley stares at Jonathan. "Aren't you running for office?"

Jonathan smiles. "That's right."

"I didn't recognize you, with the mask and everything."

"Of course not," says Jonathan.

"Well, I guess a rescue mission won't hurt your campaign."

Jonathan laughs. "I suppose you're right, but you needn't worry about that. Your privacy is more important. Can I ask why your father was trying to fight this on his own?"

"I don't know. He's been working for this company for thirty years. He's loyal. We don't exactly see eye-to-eye on his career, but he wasn't about to change it now. Like he said, it put me through school and gave us a good life. That was his real motivation."

Jonathan smiles. "Things really aren't black and white, I suppose. Even the wildlife don't seem to know what they're doing."

"What did you see?" asks Ashley.

"Caribou. We stopped to get some pictures of a northern herd that was boxed in. They were distressed and desperate, running over the Hart ranges."

"You saw caribou?"

"Yes. Jay was getting photos for an environmental campaign he's working on. As you may know, it's important to me as well."

"Yes, I do respect your views. I'm with the wildlife department. I have been tracking the herd for years. You're right, they are desperate. It appears our government is putting great effort into their extinction. I have been tracking their travel patterns for several years now. Since the new compressor site went in, they've been forced to change habitats.

"We've managed to create a stress response so great that animals are doing whatever they can to adapt. The noise and light pollution from these sites alone have forced the animals to live on less food and travel further to find it. They have to spend more time traveling than they do eating. Even the songbirds have been forced out because they can no longer hear their potential mates.

"I see you are passionate about your work as well. Unfortunately, mankind's zone of influence has no bounds," says Jonathan. He looks at Douglas. "That must make for some interesting dinner conversations."

"Indeed," says Ashley. She gives her father another drink of water.

"Chelsey General straight ahead," says Paul. He notifies the hospital of their approach. "Roger that, thank you. We're clear to land." He carefully navigates to the helipad and Jay opens the door.

"Good luck to you and your father," says Jay.

"Thank you again," says Ashley.

Jonathan helps Ashley in with her father as Jay and Paul watch from the chopper. She thanks him with a hug as paramedics roll her father into the hospital. Jonathan runs back to the chopper and puts on his headset.

"OK, let's fuel up and get out of here."

"Roger that," says Paul.

They quickly gain elevation and head back to the west coast.

Jonathan's mind is flooded with contradiction. Talk about a foolish endeavour, protecting the oil industry. What did Douglas think was going to happen? He was just trying to be a good father, a provider, and obviously raised his children with pride.

Where did humanity go wrong? When did it become human nature to always want more, to the point of destruction?

His incessant self-talk is interrupted by a smug voice in his ear.

"Hey, Jonathan!" says Jay.

"Yes?"

"I thought you weren't going to make any friends."

Jonathan looks at a smiling Jay and Paul, who are clearly sharing some irony at his expense. Jonathan smirks. "Yes, imagine that for unintended consequences."

"Well, it is an ominous new world on the horizon," Jay says with a sigh.

"Yes, it is, my friend. It certainly is," says Jonathan.

The Downtown East Side

In the rain-soaked alleyway behind the old Colonial Hotel a blue tarp is thrown over two overflowing dumpsters. Wedged in between are pieces of cardboard separating the Director's body from the cold, hard ground. One of the Colonial's bar staff is finishing his smoke break. He relieves himself on the damp earth and slams the back door as he reenters the building.

The Director slowly straightens his broken body and rises from his concrete bed. The smell of fresh urine permeates the wet ground.

"Christ, do you have to piss where a man is sleeping?" he yells into the emptiness. His attention moves to the discarded cigarette butt. He fumbles forward, carefully reaching for the brown scrap. "Ah, there's life left in you yet."

A mound of cotton and fleece next to him stirs. "What is it? You got somethin'?"

The Director does not reply. He is focused on his find. He picks up the butt, clips it with his stained fingertips, cups it with his free hand, and falls back against the old building, returning to his haunches.

A wide-eyed Henry smiles under his dripping hood of matted fur.

"Told you! I told you this was a good spot." Taking credit for the find.

The Director drags on the butt like an infant's first latch. He fills his lungs as deeply as they will allow, holds his moment of bliss, then expels a cloud of smoke and hands it to his friend.

Henry sucks so hard on the morsel that he burns his lips. "Fuck!" he chokes, throwing it back to the street.

The Director bends forward in a choking giggle. "You eatin' it? They're not that tasty." He chuckles.

"Shut your rotten pie hole," Henry replies.

"You can have the next one, if you're awake," the Director says. He struggles to his feet. "Now come on. We have to make our way to Hastings."

"Hastings!" Henry squawks, shuffling forward. "It's crowded over there. So many now you can't get a place to lay your head."

"Stop your bawling! Them homeless are no different than us, running from something and barred from somewhere else. Besides, I told you yesterday, I have to pick a pig."

Henry stops and scans his friend's weathered brown face for an answer. He's known the Director for most of his life, though not as a friend. Richard James Roberts does not make friends; he is too busy surviving to bother with niceties like friendship.

RJ, as he is called, is known mostly by reputation. For most Indigenous people born in the twentieth century, life began way behind the start line and survival demands you dodge as much of it as you can. RJ has always been busy running, hiding, defending himself, and justifying his existence—essential skills for kids raised in a world where the term "adverse experience" is not only ordinary but accepted.

RJ and his younger brother were two of an estimated one hundred and fifty thousand Indigenous children corralled by Canadian Indian agents under the auspices of the Indian Act. They were penned into residential schools, where they spent much of their school years learning to deny who they really were.

People who knew RJ said he could take the worst lashings the supervisors dished out, but his younger brother was not of the same cut. RJ said his brother Robbie was heartsick. The staff in charge refused to let them see each other. Cutting family ties was an important step in the rebranding. They cut Robbie's hair and doled out lashings for speaking his native language. RJ said they tried to wash the Indian out of them, and Robbie was dying of shock, so RJ got them out.

Despite months of searching, the boys were never found. Rumours were that the pair ended up in the foster system, but no one knew for sure, until two years later, when a weathered bandit showed up on the lower east side after losing a last-chance job "due to intoxication."

A broken and usually drunken RJ can often be heard spewing, like projectile vomit, bits and pieces of the horrors lived by him and his brother.

"Living nightmares," he'd call the cultural washing.

Images of children being robbed of their families, languages, and traditions saturate RJ's consciousness, especially at night. Sleep does not come easily. The only healing afforded to him is the numbing kind. And RJ partakes regularly.

Henry and a few other familiar faces have asked about his life after the Alberni residential school. But for survival purposes, the Director doesn't like to remember.

After escaping the school, RJ and his brother ended up back in the hands of the government, and a defiant RJ refused to comply with the Ministry's rules. He vowed to never be controlled again. He reclaimed himself, an unwashed Indian, and swore to direct his own life. From that moment on, he was crowned the Director of Unwashed Indians, or the Director for short.

"Pick a pig, pick a pig," Henry mumbles, and then, with a flutter of recognition, it comes. "Today, pick a pig?"

The Director watches the old man's brain scrambling for the memory. "Today!" he says.

Henry restarts, and the two shuffle forward together. "Pick a pig day," he mumbles again. "If there's a pig worth picking."

A Legacy

"Stop crying, Lisa. You have to be quiet!"

Sixteen-year-old Jimmy Richards is kneeling in the surf, frantically washing his sister's hands and sleeves. She gulps and chokes on an unexpected rush of surf. As fear fills every inch of her thin body, she acquiesces, goes limp, and coughs out the cold sea.

"What happened, Jimmy?" she asks, quivering. "What happened to him? What did you do?"

"You better keep your mouth shut about it or I'll have to go away. Is that what you want?"

Lisa startles out of her sleep and sits upright in her bed. Her eyes are wide, and she is breathing hard.

"Oh, my Jimmy," she whispers. "You're still with me."

She looks around her luxurious room and can see light peeking in from behind the heavy blue silk curtains. A hand reaches for her in the dim room.

"Are you OK?"

"Yes, yes," she says. "I'm OK. It was a dream."

A sleepy Jake smiles and pulls her back down to the mattress. "It's Saturday. We don't have to get up." He kisses her and pulls her close.

"Hmm, you are very tempting, sir, but I have to get to headquarters. We have so much to do."

She jumps back up, pushes her feet into her slippers, and grabs her robe.

"Right, it's a big day," says Jake. He struggles to alertness.

"Yes," she mumbles while brushing her teeth. She spits and turns back to him. "A big day." She giggles and jumps back on the bed. She gives her husband one last kiss, scurries back to the bathroom, and begins to dress.

Two hours later, Lisa finishes a seven-kilometre run, showers, and heads downtown with a round of coffee. She parks the car and walks down the block to the two-story gabled building she has come to frequent. She stops and admires the bold black signage—Richards Headquarters—which she meticulously designed herself. It pops on the red brick frontage.

The old building is one of many on Gerrard Street that have been reclaimed and restored to their former glory. The interior is red brick and wooden beams, with contemporary neutrals in white and sand, all meticulously picked by Lisa. A bank of windows lines the front, and one large round window can be seen from the second-floor loft.

As the candidate's sister, Lisa has been instrumental to the campaign. Her training in communications and public relations for a high-tech solutions company has been an asset in every way, while her skill in painting and artistry give them an edge in a visual world.

She is energized by the sunshine and her smiling assistant, who is rushing to open the door.

"Good morning, Alyssa," says Lisa, beaming.

"Good morning, Lisa. I suppose you've been up for hours."

"Yes, it's a perfect day and I'm so excited I barely slept a wink."

"You're in good company. Look at these guys!" says Alyssa.

The office feels like a movie set. Hopes are high and the energy is contagious. Workers zigzag around the room, making final calls, coordinating car rides, writing scripts, rehearsing sound bites, and planning interviews and after-parties. Lisa has never seen such a committed crew. They love their candidate, and it shows. He handpicked every one of them—a tip passed on by his predecessor, Christopher Stamer.

"You have to know the people working with you," he used to say. "If they share your vision, they know you're worth fighting for, and together you create a powerful movement."

Jonathan and Lisa witnessed first-hand how passion and momentum can grow for a common cause, particularly one that puts people and planet first. At first, they thought the statement was ridiculously simple, but later recognized the complexity of the slogan. The simplicity and humanity of the message strips bare a painful reality: People and planet have never taken the front seat, as Rosa Parks bravely pointed out. White privilege, big business, and greed have been driving the bus.

Jonathan was at Stamer's side through two successful elections, learning the logistics of a successful campaign and the principles of the game. Stamer stood as a voice for the voiceless. He witnessed the over-policing of minorities, where minor offences delivered a life of hardship for the poor and underprivileged. He used Jonathan's case as the cornerstone to prove that positive outcomes are more likely when youth justice focuses on relationship-building and community support. He passed many of his values and his passion for social issues onto his apprentice.

Jonathan was devastated when his beloved mentor succumbed to a life-long heart condition. The "ticking time bomb", as Stamer called it, gave its last beat three weeks before he was set to retire. Jonathan wondered if it was the uncertainty of his health that gave Stamer his drive, and he debated whether he could live up to his legacy. Despite some hesitation, he was compelled to accept the challenge and pick up where Stamer left off.

Over the years, he has provided free legal counsel for Black and Indigenous youth, attended environmental calls for action, and eventually entered the world of politics. He successfully became a federal member for his district and was voted leader of the Humanitarian Green Party of Canada.

The Hum Gees really began to spark after a series of environmental and financial disasters shook the globe, pushing more and more working and middle class people into the fringes—a place no one ever expects to be, until they are. People were shaken to their core. Unrest and social movements grew, and the party gained momentum among people from all races who were disillusioned by the state of the world. Blatant racism and a deteriorating planet can have a strong impact when fear sets in. When you can't safely leave your home or breathe the air, it begs the question: Who's been in charge?

"Where is he?" asks Lisa.

Alyssa smiles and points to the back office. Lisa hands her a coffee from the tray and heads to the back.

Jonathan is on the phone. He smiles at his sister as she enters and brightens like a pup when he sees her offering.

"Thank you, I appreciate that. Will you be by tonight? Great, that's great. I look forward to it. No matter how it goes, I am so grateful you will be here. That's right, just the beginning. OK, see you soon." He hangs up the phone. "Hey, sis!"

"Whatever way it goes? What are you saying, bro? You know you got this!"

Jonathan smiles. "I love you, sis. Always the optimist, and toting coffee from Cloudberry. What a treat!"

"Well, I thought you should have your favourite today, and Molly wants us to confirm the breakfast on Friday morning. They have it all planned. You and Bethany can dodge in the back door if you want. I like the idea of having it on this block where we've worked so hard. It will be a great place for a celebratory breakfast!"

Jonathan laughs. "OK, now you're just being cocky."

"Did you finish your speech?" she asks.

Jonathan nods with a smile.

"Can I look at it?" she asks.

"I'm counting on it." He hands her a folder with his carefully crafted words, which he spent most of the night composing.

"Let me know what you think."

The phone rings, and Lisa leaves the room with the script clutched tight to her chest.

"Hello?" Jonathan says. "Yes, Bernice. OK, thank you. Is he all settled in? That's wonderful. I will see him in an hour or so. I'm looking forward to it too."

Jonathan makes his way through the busy headquarters, checking in with each of the logistical volunteers for the day, and makes his way to the second floor, where Lisa is deeply focused on her reading.

He ducks his head into her office. "Is it any good?"

"Yes, it is. I think you've nailed it. It's authentic, it's intelligent, it's you."

"Well, thank you, sister. Now grab your coat. We have a stop to make. Daiji's in town!"

Little Vietnam

The Director and Henry make their way around people, carts, bikes, and tarps on East Hastings.

"Like dodging landmines," says Henry.

Little Vietnam stretches for four blocks in an area around the intersection of East Hastings and Columbia Street on the downtown east side of Vancouver. The collective last stop for the abandoned, abused, substance-dependant, and mentally ill. Any visitor to this hell must choose their steps wisely so as to not disturb anyone's shelter or step on a needle.

"Meth head." The Director steps over a body wrapped in a tarp on the sidewalk.

"Their day is different than ours," says Henry. "Their hits keep them up most of the night, so sleep comes during the day."

The Director nods. He understands the story. He and Henry discussed the matter at length while deep into their own substance-induced psychosis and concluded that it wasn't a bad way to go. Less chance of freezing at night.

Despite the alarming statistics of drug use, rape, and crime, the residents of the downtown east side have a certain camaraderie among them. Their faces can't hide the burden of shame and sadness they each carry, and for a short time, the weight of it disperses among them in a bond of silent understanding before turning into suspicion and fear.

The Director and Henry scavenge a few more cigarette butts and coins and stop into Pete's Convenience and Liquor. They have been saving and scrounging for days, collecting enough for twenty-six ounces of black spirit. Their first purchase in days. The third week of the month is always the hardest, because the money's all gone, and begging and scrounging is the only way through. With a little change left, the Director stops at Nancy's Souvenirs and buys a pair of plastic shades for fifty cents.

He dons his new purchase and looks at Henry. "What ya think, Henry? Am I sophisticated now?"

"Yes, sir, a real Stevie Wonder," says Henry.

"Nancy's tweaking is bad this morning," says the Director.

"God bless her," says Henry. "She needs to stop that poison."

They share their brown-bagged courage while scanning the block for the best chance at breakfast. The lineup outside the Good Samaritan is already substantial, but looks like it's moving, at least. Henry caps off the bottle and stashes the brown bag under his layers.

The Director has a burst of motivation from his morning cocktail. "Let's try here, Henry, and then head to the square. There's something I need to do."

"What's at the square?" asks Henry.

"He's doing a speech there. The new guy."

"Since when do you care about picking pigs? You can't trust 'em. They aren't helping us none."

"I know, Henry, but some are better than others. I didn't go through the trouble of registering at the centre for nothing. Do you remember that, Henry?"

"Yes. I remember that day. It was a shit of a day, waiting to prove who you was."

"Well, I didn't go through all that for nothing. Now I'm gonna pick a pig. A good pig."

"But there ain't no good ones!" Henry drones.

"There is one good one, Henry."

"Who is this one?"

"This one could be different and he's gonna be at the square."

"Ha!" says Henry. "There ain't no exceptions, unless he's Jesus. Is he Jesus? 'Cause some think he's an exception, but I don't. I don't believe Jesus is any better than the rest of us. Why would we be lining up here, waiting and waiting, if Jesus was an exception? Jesus didn't help us in them schools."

"I'm not talking about Jesus, Henry. You can see for yourself. Do what you want! Pick a pig, don't pick a pig. I really don't care, Henry. Now, let's get some food before my belly starts eating my backbone."

Henry laughs. "Yes, let's just put a pig on our plate."

"A nice crispy one."

Final Arrangements

Jonathan and Lisa leave West Hastings and merge into the downtown traffic. They make their way toward the waterfront and Harbour View Hotel, where Lisa has reserved a suite for election night. Daiji also has a room there. Jonathan insisted his mentor come for the evening. Daiji has always been a source of inspiration for Jonathan, and now that Jonah and Mary have passed, his presence is needed more than ever.

Daiji was more than happy to be included.

"I can't wait to see him," says Lisa. "How's his health?"

"Bernice says he's as sharp as ever. At ninety-two, he's the same insightful shaman he's always been."

Jonathan and Lisa check into their room to ensure everything is in place for tomorrow night. The spacious penthouse suite is perfect for tomorrow night's festivities. A wall of windows overlooks the harbour, with a patio door and balcony for a breezier view. A baby grand is poised in the corner and a fully stocked kitchen is prepped for the night's celebrations. Jonathan was not comfortable with the lavish digs, but was convinced it may be a safer bet than the downtown headquarters in a controversial election.

Jonathan makes a call to Daiji's room. Bernice answers and relays a message to Jonathan. Daiji's gone for a quick walk in the park with Barbara but should be back shortly.

Jonathan and Lisa sit in the luxurious leather wingbacks and admire the view of the harbour.

"You know, Jonathan," says Lisa, "whichever way this goes, you absolutely have to see this as a huge success. The campaign has gained momentum. You've given people a vision of what's possible. You have upped the ante, so to speak. This is huge! People are no longer willing to accept mismanagement and inequality. It's been a long time coming. Look at where we started. It could have been so different for us. You could have been so different."

"I know it. That's why it's so important to have Daiji here. I just wish—" Jonathan stops himself.

"I know what you wish, honey. I know."

"It's been such a long time. I wish he was with us. We don't even know if he's dead or alive," says Jonathan.

"I know, Jonathan. I was so young. I can't even begin to understand what happened."

Jonathan sighs. "We were just curious, innocent kids."

The Journey Back

Ten-year-old Lisa Richards takes off her socks and shoes and runs with her arms outstretched, like a shorebird, between the surf and sand of Nora Beach.

"Tweet, tweet, tweet!"

Her two older brothers laugh and run with her.

"Let's go see the medicine man," says Jimmy.

Jonathan stops. "Who?" he asks.

Jimmy points in the distance. "See the teepee? A medicine man lives there. I spoke to him before."

"Are we allowed?" asks Jonathan.

"Who's going to stop us?" says Jimmy.

Jonathan shrugs. "OK."

"Lisa!" Jonathan waves to his sister, who is halfway down the beach.

Lisa stops and reluctantly chases after her brothers, who are already making their way to the teepee. She catches up just before they knock at the canvas door.

"Hello, Jimmy. Come in," says a voice from within.

The shaman welcomes the three children. He is wearing a black T-shirt and soft cotton pants. His whole face smiles and he welcomes them to sit on the cushions on the floor.

Jonathan and Lisa look around the round structure. The man tells them his name is Daiji. The surfers built the teepee for him.

He shows them the drawings of surfers, the sea, and a man in a canoe on the canvas. He explains the drawings are a story of when he was a young man.

The teepee has a hole in the top and a small fire is burning. There is a bed made of wood and foam with a red fleece blanket. He has several yellow and green cushions for sitting and there are carvings and drawings pinned to the wall. He shows the children a carving he is working on today. He hands it to Lisa.

"It's a whale!" she says, smiling.

"Yes," says Daiji.

"Let me see," says Jonathan, reaching for it.

The medicine man turns his attention to Jimmy. "I haven't seen you for a while, Jimmy. How are you doing?"

"I'm OK," says Jimmy.

Lisa and Jonathan are surprised by the familiarity.

"Do you know Jimmy?" asks Lisa.

"Yes, we met before," Daiji says. "Are you all family?"

"Yes, these are my brothers," says Lisa.

"How very nice for you," he says. "Jimmy tells me you are from Tla-o-qui-aht Nation. Do you live close by?"

Jimmy interrupts before Lisa can answer. "We live in Ramsey, just downtown," he lies.

Jonathan and Lisa look puzzled, but dare not question their brother's motives.

"Do you have a big family?" Daiji continues.

Jonathan shoots a look at his brother, who is becoming increasingly restless.

"What is your family name?" Daiji asks. "Maybe I know of your parents."

Jimmy is not answering. He looks numb and his eyes are hollow.

"Are you part of the Nuu-chah-nulth Nation, like me?"

Daiji continues to speak. Lisa freezes, knowing the questions will be difficult to answer. Her brothers changed their names and don't like to talk about family.

Jimmy jumps up and yells, "Why all the questions? You don't know our parents and it's none of your business, anyway!"

The man is startled by the sudden reaction and jumps to his feet. He reaches out to Jimmy in a kind gesture of regret. "I'm sorry, Jimmy. I didn't mean to."

Jimmy doesn't allow him to finish. He pushes him, but the man resists and places his hands on Jimmy's shoulders.

"No, Jimmy, please."

Jimmy doesn't hear him. He only hears the questions. More questions. He thinks they are orphans. He is deciding they are no good. Jimmy's mind is racing. Why does this man have to ruin their family? He has to stop it, or his siblings will be taken away. He punches, kicks, and screams. A body falls.

Jimmy takes a knife from his sock and stabs at the canvas walls, yelling, stabbing, kicking. He doesn't know where he is, but he understands the danger. He has to protect his siblings. He must fight. He continues to scream and destroy the teepee until the canvas hangs in shreds and the logs begin to fall. Lisa is bent over the man, wiping his face and crying.

Jonathan drags Lisa off him and yells at Jimmy. "Jimmy, stop! We have to run now." Jonathan takes Lisa's hand and pulls her out of the teepee.

What has happened? Why are they running? Jimmy is in a cold sweat. His head is pounding and he can hear his heart beating. He's certain it will explode. He looks at the man on the ground. Daiji's head is bleeding and the canvas is catching fire. He grabs Daiji's arms and begins pulling, but he can't budge him. It's the logs, he's trapped!

Jimmy pushes one of the large beams with both hands, catching one of his sleeves. He frantically douses the flame with his other hand, searing his skin. He drags the man across the floor and out of the hut.

A shocked Lisa is crying, looking at the blood on her pink shirt. Jimmy pulls her to the water while Jonathan looks for the shoes she left on the beach.

"Stop crying, Lisa. You have to be quiet!"

Jimmy is kneeling in the surf, frantically washing Lisa's hands and sleeves. He has to act fast. Think smart, be calm, figure this out. His aggression drags Lisa onto her belly, grinding her chin on the sand. She gulps and chokes on an unexpected rush of the surf. As fear fills every inch of her thin body, she goes limp and coughs out the cold sea. Jimmy calms his voice and smooths his sister's pink tunic with the yellow flowers, as if to restore it to the clean, dry version she proudly donned this morning.

"What happened, Jimmy?" she asks, quivering. "What happened to him? What did you do?"

"I didn't do anything," he shoots back. "It was an accident! It wasn't my fault, Lisa! You better keep your mouth shut about it or I'll have to go away. Is that what you want?"

Lisa sobs quietly. "Where's Jonathan?" she asks.

A voice bends to her ear. "I'm here, Lisa. It's OK. We're OK."

Jonathan places her small, cold hand in his, bringing her instant comfort. Jonathan pulls her in, helps put on her shoes, and hugs her. He scowls at his older brother. Jonathan brings Lisa a calm reassurance. A skill she has come to count on.

"We have to go," Jimmy commands. "We have to take the tracks. Grab her, Jonathan."

"What about him? What if there's a train?" Jonathan yells after him.

Jonathan helps Lisa up from the beach and tries to keep up with his big brother's pace. Jimmy stops and stares at them.

"We have no choice! We have to go now!" He heads for the track. "There is no train coming. We can make it. If it comes, we'll jump."

The two kilometres of railroad track between Nora Beach and Shannon House follow a narrow cliffside with a twenty foot drop on either side, making jumping a last resort.

Lisa digs in her heels. "No, not the tracks. Please, Jimmy, Jonathan, I can't."

Jonathan grabs Lisa's arms and swings her onto his back. "I got you, Lisa. You're safe with me."

The three scurry across the tracks, toward the setting sun, as smoke billows in the distance.

Getting Past Eugene

Jimmy, Jonathan, and Lisa avoid train traffic, but getting past Eugene will be more difficult. Eugene just started his night shift at Shannon House and is helping Lindsay with snacks in the kitchen. Jimmy will have to distract him while Jonathan gets Lisa to her room. Jimmy rolls up his sleeves, hiding the charred fabric. His skin burns and is turning red. Eugene stops Jimmy while an exhausted Jonathan helps Lisa to her room.

"You're back, and just in the nick of time," Eugene says. "It's getting late. Where's Lisa?"

Jimmy puts his hands in his pockets. "She's here, everything's fine. Jonathan is taking her to her room." He tries to keep his distance from Eugene while distracting him from Jonathan and Lisa. "Can I make some popcorn?" asks Jimmy. He looks in the cupboard.

Lisa follows her orders and rushes to her room with a doting Jonathan behind her. His arms are sore from anchoring her on his back. He imagines hers must be, too. He helps her find her pyjamas.

"As soon as you're dressed, get in bed and turn off the light," he says, backing out of the room.

"Jonathan!"

"What?" he whispers.

"Are we going to be OK?"

"Yes, we will be fine. Just remember what we said. We were at the park, OK?"

"OK," she says. She turns off the light and burrows into her covers.

Jonathan can still hear Eugene and Jimmy. Jimmy is a master of distraction. Playing smart and acting cool are well-developed skills. He's probably getting snacks and laughing it up with the others.

Jonathan walks past them. "Good night," he says, waving his hand.

Eugene peeks out from the kitchen to catch a glimpse of him. "Everything OK, Jonathan?"

"Yes."

"Where's Lisa?"

"She's in bed. She's tired. We shouldn't have had her out so late."

"That's right, Jonathan, you shouldn't have," Eugene says. "We will talk about it tomorrow."

"OK, Eugene, I'm tired too. I'm going to play some games in my room."

"OK, good night," shouts Eugene.

Jonathan makes his way to his room and closes the door. As he undresses, sand falls to the floor. He shoves it under the bed with his foot. He unbuttons his pants, and something drops from his pocket. He picks up the tiny whale carving. He brushes it off and puts it under his pillow.

"We're sorry," he says. He turns off the light. "He didn't mean it. He never really means it."

Full Circle

A knock on the hotel room door jars Jonathan and Lisa out of their hypnotic journey to the past. Lisa straightens her clothes and stands. Jonathan answers the door. Daiji's warm smile and bright eyes greet him. He bows to Jonathan.

"Daiji!" says Jonathan.

"My heart," says Daiji.

The two men embrace for a long time.

"Jonathan, stop monopolizing our guest," says Lisa.

Jonathan laughs. "Do you remember this nuisance, Daiji?"

"Yes. Yes, I do," he says, reaching out to hug her. "It's very nice to see you."

"Come in, Daiji. Please sit. I'll get you something to drink. What would you like? I have your favourite tea."

"Yes, thank you, Jonathan."

Jonathan, Lisa, and Daiji sit and reminisce about their days together in Clayoquot Sound, the lessons they learned from Christopher Stamer, the pending election, and Jonathan's upcoming appearance in the square tonight.

Lisa breaks from the jovial reminiscing with a deep sigh. She has been working tirelessly with Jonathan for months preparing for this campaign, and for a moment, she looks apprehensive. A look Jonathan does not recognize in his sister.

"What is it, Lisa? Are you worried about the speech? The results, maybe?"

"No, no. I mean, we've done our best. If the people are ready for change, it will be. If not, we work on our own, like we have been all along."

"That's right, sis," says Jonathan. "That's what we do."

Daiji senses something deeper lingering in Lisa's thoughts. "What's on your mind, Lisa?" he asks.

"OK, here it goes," she says.

Jonathan gives a concerned look.

"There's something I need to know. Something neither of you have fully explained to me about that night. The night we first met."

Daiji smiles, anticipating Lisa's line of thought.

"Daiji, just before you arrived, Lisa and I were doing some very heavy soul searching," Jonathan says. "I have been thinking about Jimmy."

"It's not just Jimmy, Jonathan," says Lisa. "It's about you and Daiji.

Why did you do what you did, Jonathan? Daiji, you went along with it. I mean, it all turned out for the best, thank God. I understand it was a blessing. But you didn't tell me why you took the fall for Jimmy. I was there. Daiji was there. Jimmy hurt Daiji, not you!"

Daiji closes his eyes with a slight smile and allows Jonathan to explain.

"You're right, Lisa. I didn't explain. We were so young, and I didn't realize you were having these thoughts. As you know, before Jimmy and I were reunited with you in Ramsey, we were on the run for a while. He broke me out of the Alberni residential school. I was slowly dying there, and I know that if Jimmy hadn't done what he did, I would not be here right now. He was all that I had.

"We spent days in the woods before we found Uncle Bernie's cabin. Jimmy fed me, kept me warm. He kept me alive! When they took us from our uncle, we were fortunate enough to be reunited with you, but Jimmy was having a difficult time. Jimmy was also terribly abused in that place. He was stronger than me. Part of me thinks that because he was being strong for me, caring for me, and getting me out, he wasn't thinking of his own pain. I don't think he even realized he had pain. He spent so much time pushing it back. You see, no one took care of him. He was always taking care of me.

"What Jimmy did to Daiji was not right. It was terrible and I have nightmares about it, but I've had years to think about this. I think Jimmy was triggered by something and he thought he was back at Alberni.

"He has been a fighter his entire life and was always in survival mode. That takes a toll on a kid. I thought it was time for me to rescue him. I knew the consequences would be lighter for me and he deserved to get away this time. I didn't understand all of this back then, but my gut told me it was the right thing to do.

"We were so blessed. I am grateful we were given a second chance and had all these wonderful opportunities bestowed upon us by Daiji and Mr. Stamer and the Tla-o-qui-aht community. Still, part of me feels it's so unfair that Jimmy did not receive the same gifts we did."

Daiji opens his eyes.

"You are right, Jonathan," he says. "Your brother has been through a lot. You all have. He really believed he had to fight me in the teepee. You don't give yourself enough credit, though. You forgave Jimmy for leaving. The compassion you hold for your brother changed the world for you, Jonathan. It wasn't me or Christopher. You did it. The way you respond to the world has the power to lift you higher. Your act of admission woke me from my sleep, filling me with gratitude. It was easy for me to accept your story, as it was an extraordinary act of courage. Your life has been flowing from that kindness ever since. You have touched us all, Jonathan.

"You believe Jimmy hasn't had the same gifts you and Lisa were given, but he has, Jonathan. You are Jimmy's gift to the world. He helped create you. Now, you have been put in a position to help a lot of people. That couldn't have happened without his help.

"Most people still act as though their behaviours don't affect others. That we are all separate. You have the opportunity to teach them that we must work together if we are going to save this planet and raise all our brothers and sisters out of poverty. You have a chance to show them the power of their choices. These synchronistic events could not have happened without your courage."

"Or without your love and forgiveness," says Jonathan. "Thank you, Daiji. I wish there was some way he could know that. I hope I can make him proud."

"He knows, Jonathan."

Lisa smiles and wipes her eyes. "Thank you both," she says. "Well, brother, you can make us all proud by getting ready for that speech. We have to make our way to the square."

"Oh, yes, about that. I have been talking to my security team."

"Oh, good," says Lisa.

"Yes, and I have decided to take the subway to Victory Square."

"The subway? Jonathan, why?"

"I take the subway. The people I represent take the subway. I want to feel the energy there."

"How does Bethany feel about it?" asks Lisa.

"She understands. She'll go to the square with you and Jake. I will see you there."

"And your security?"

"Agent Marshall is not happy, but she agreed. They will be with me every step of the way."

"Be careful, Jonathan. Daiji will come with us. Remember, just be yourself and you cannot lose."

"Thanks, Lisa."

"Daiji, I will be back to get you at three," says Lisa.

The City Pulse

Hastings Station is jammed. The labyrinth at the city centre hosts an average of five thousand commuters, tourists, runaways, and performers every day, but today it will be double that. Today, they come in droves from all corners of the Greater Vancouver Area and beyond, eagerly thrusting themselves into a vortex of pulsating emotion. The outraged hold banners, the peaceful hold hands, some pace, some chant, all making a plea. Some are desperate to turn the tide while others remain firmly planted. Either way, this is a last-ditch effort.

Agent Gillian Marshall weaves and bobs through human traffic on her way to one of the biggest security details of the decade. She purposely entered the fray to get a sense of the tension heading east, and possibly cut off trouble before it starts. Problem is, she wasn't expecting to have company. This last-minute request from the controversial star candidate to step into the busiest subway portal in the city is nothing short of ludicrous, changing her mission from recon to pure defence. Now she travels with three other agents as a visible escort, armed and in uniform. Four high security members poised for modern warfare. Marshall, Cortez, Smith, and Yung are experienced in high-level protection and tasked with ensuring the candidate arrives safely.

Marshall retrieves her cell phone and makes a call. "We're fifteen minutes out. How's it shaping up? What about the square? How far back?"

She stops in her tracks and is almost rear-ended by a protester with a placard reading "People and Planet." He screeches to a stop and scowls. She waves him on. The candidate has been spotted and people rush to get a glimpse. A palpable shift races in their direction and a chorus of chanting begins.

"Black lives matter! Black lives matter!"

The Black Lives Matter movement has reached unprecedented heights. It is no longer a flickering hope from a few patient souls, but rather a forceful demand that will not be ignored. They are well represented—Black Canadians, Indigenous people, and minorities of every colour. Those who have not been well served by society. Interspersed among them, people hold slogans for Humanitarian Green Party, which claims to put people and planet first.

They rush the security detail, pointing phones in a frenzy of video-shooting, photo-snapping, and attention-grabbing. They move onto the platform. Agent Marshall pulls Jonathan closer to her side. The team members position themselves to protect and defend if necessary.

A masked protestor shouts from across the track, "Wagon burner!"

The team pauses and forms a protective shield around the candidate. The white supremacists have also come to make their stand. A handful skulk around the periphery, camouflaging their skinned heads, while others lurk under politically correct banners. Their "Keep Canada Strong" campaign feigns support for middle-class wage earners while harbouring sentiments of colour-specific nativism. They are bullies, fuelled by accustomed wealth, status, and obtuse white privilege.

"Twelve o'clock across the track!" shouts Yang.

"Are they armed?" asks Smith. He stands on high alert.

"Can't tell." Yang quickly zooms in on the likely suspects. "Don't think so. Just a little flexing."

"Leave it for the Vancouver PD," Marshall shouts. "Stay on mission."

"It doesn't look like a threat," says Smith.

"It's Canada. The assholes have free speech," says Cortez.

"Sticks and stones," replies Marshall. "Let the locals keep an eye out." She speaks into her headset. "Vancouver PD, we have a small group of six to eight aggressive protestors. Black hoodies, face masks, shouting racial slurs, no visible weapons."

"Don't mean they're not there," adds Cortez.

"Vancouver PD, we really don't know if they pose a threat. We have it covered here, but you might want to take a look. We are about to board," says Marshall.

"Roger that," the radio responds.

Jonathan feels charged by the grit and desperation of the crowd. He falls in line with the security detail, but his mind is busy. On the eve of the election, this will be a vital appeal. One he planned himself. Nowhere has the collapse of the social security net been more felt than in the poorest streets of this country. He has never been so sure of where he needs to be.

The media hype surrounding the event has predicted a good turnout, and if the bobbing placards and painted faces in the downtown station are any indication, they may be right. It won't be an easy race. By holding the highest office in the Canadian government, the incumbent has a perilous advantage: the support of the purse-string holders. His chokehold on money and influence is unwavering, and his lack of morality is convenient in a world that favours scapegoating and fearmongering over environmental responsibility or poverty reduction. Anyone who doesn't put forward an agenda favouring tax-cutting, big business, and survival of the fittest is fair game to be steamrolled.

Despite the odds, Jonathan is counting on the one thing that money can't cover up: an unprecedented desperation in the air. A desperation based on the unravelling of a system that spent too much time sustaining the wealth of the rich while putting the environment and poverty on hold.

The imbalance has reached its tipping point. If the current government continues to endorse fossil fuel industries and bow to big business, emission reduction targets won't be met, recovery will be impossible, social programs will be overburdened, homelessness will increase, and recommendations for health care will go unheeded. The majority will suffer.

An incoming train roars into the station, its wheels squealing and sparking to a stop.

"This is our train," Marshall says.

She stretches her arm out in front of Jonathan, nudging him back. The car doors open and the six of them step inside, claiming sole occupation of the front car. Two team members flank the doors, blocking access from adjoining cars, while Marshall stands in front of the candidate.

"You OK?" she asks.

"Never better," he replies. "This is inspiring!"

"What do you mean?" she asks, bewildered. She's still choked by the unnecessary risk and security demand.

"Did you see those people?" he asks.

"Yes. I heard them, too. Not everyone is your friend, Jonathan."

"I don't expect them to be, Gillian. People have the right to protest. Change frightens them and they see it coming. People care how this turns out because now more than ever, the outcome will affect their lives. Every voice matters."

"It also increases risk. As long as you understand that!" she says. "Things are getting pretty bad down here. The east side is about to explode, and it's moving west. Industries are shutting down, homeless numbers are up, and our ability to care for them has decreased. It's not about politics anymore. This screams survival."

"You are absolutely right," says Jonathan. For once, we have to work together as a majority. Otherwise this whole house of cards collapses."

Jonathan swivels around and faces the security team. His appeal is alluring. His warm brown eyes and sincere smile are housed within an extraordinary container of wise, gentle confidence. The star candidate has an undeniable authenticity to him. He speaks with candour borne out of experience, not all of which he gained politely. The mere fact that he escaped the pull of bitterness in favour of change, education, and perseverance is formidable in and of itself. His history prevents idealism, but his experience fuels pure grit.

"The people have spoken. Hell, they're screaming! We need a big change."

"What makes you think you can do that? No one has been able to yet. That's a tall order," says Cortez.

"You are so right. It is a tall order," says Jonathan. "It requires a step out of the ordinary way of doing things. We have to choose with intent, respond in a conscious way, a compassionate way. Until now, very few have. Take the example in the US a few years ago—the children at the US border who were separated from their parents. Some of them were lost to the unjust, tyrannical actions of an uninformed leader. Consequently, these children were set up for a lifetime of hardship. They escaped one country to seek asylum in another, and if the people in that administration had opened their eyes and looked at the situation through the filter of decency and kindness, and come up with solutions that were humanitarian-based as opposed to greed-based, things could be different for them. They would still be with their families, not running afraid, as they are now."

"What makes you think things would be better for them now?" asks Yang.

Jonathan smiles. "Don't underestimate your power to change a life. One kind act, one act beyond an ordinary, humdrum reaction, can change someone's life forever. You only need to observe the trajectory of your own life. Who influenced you the most? Who brought you fear and who gave you hope? Each of us is responsible for changing the world. That's the shift that is taking place now."

Ray Cortez is from an immigrant Canadian family, and he's a veteran on the team. He jumped at the opportunity to lead the detail out of respect for the candidate. "Are you practicing your speech, sir?" he asks.

"How's it sound?" Jonathan asks with a wink.

The team breaks out into laughter.

A Vision and a Speech

"OK, this is it," says Marshall.

The four agents take their positions in front of and behind Jonathan, and they all step out of the train at Victory Square. Jonathan follows the two officers in front of him and listens to Gillian issuing orders at his side, all while thinking of the key points he wants to hit.

The east side is an important district. The people here have been ignored the most, and they have the most to gain. He needs to inspire. This speech can't wait.

Outside the station, they only have to walk a few hundred metres to get to the square. They are spotted by bystanders, who walk with the group. People run up for photos, only to be pushed back by security. Some begin chanting.

"Homes for all! Homes for all!"

Some people snap photos. Jonathan slows his pace to shake hands and thank people for coming.

"Not now!" Marshall stands between Jonathan and the bystanders.

"No more contact. Just head for the stage."

"OK, Gillian OK."

Jonathan ducks behind the stage to catch his breath, drink some water, and take a look at his notes. Bethany and Lisa join him.

"Good luck, honey. You got this. We are so proud of you," says Bethany. She kisses him and Jonathan hugs her close.

"It's time," says Lisa.

Lisa and Bethany take a seat at the side of the stage, just hidden from public view. Jonathan takes one more moment in the back room and begins to breathe deep. He thinks of Stamer and everything he learned from him. He thinks of Daiji and his willingness to believe in a frightened boy. He thinks of Jimmy, who risked everything to set him free. Jonathan retrieves his carving from his pants pocket and presses it to his lips.

"This is for you," he whispers.

Hundreds of people line the sidewalks and others camp out in the square. A helicopter hovers overhead, trying to capture the phenomenal image. Journalists report live in an attempt to give everyone a taste of the enthusiastic scene.

"The outpouring of support is really unprecedented here today. We know Jonathan Richards is a popular contender, but the enthusiasm and energy of this gathering is incredible. The demographic of this crowd is diverse. This is exactly what Jonathan Richards is counting on. He says he stands for the voiceless, and he is certainly a favourite here on the east side of the city tonight."

Jonathan hears his cue. His campaign manager Hamish is beginning his introduction. "Ladies and gentlemen, thank you all for coming out on the eve of our federal election. A race that will go down in history as a game changer! You are here because you know change is in the air, and it starts with your Humanitarian Green candidate for Prime Minister of Canada: Jonathan Richards!"

Jonathan steps onto the stage. "Hello, Vancouver! I am thrilled to see you here this evening!"

The crowd cheers.

"I don't have to stress how important this election is, because I know you understand this. So much has happened in the last five years. It is a time of reckoning. What have we learned?" Jonathan pauses and looks out at the crowd. "What have we learned?"

The crowd responds. "Black lives matter! Black lives matter!"

"We have learned that Black lives matter!" Jonathan chants.

The crowd chants loudly. "Black lives matter! Black lives matter! Black lives matter!"

Jonathan continues to chant with the crowd. The air vibrates. He doesn't want to stop this sweet momentum, a momentum that has been building for what seems like lifetimes. He lets them run with it. He owes it to each one of them.

Then he begins.

"We need to embrace, learn from, and be proud of our diversity. Racism and discrimination will not be tolerated in our country! If you cannot treat us as we deserve to be treated, then you shouldn't get the job. The Humanitarian Greens call for an end to criminalization of race and the systemic exclusion of Black, brown-skinned, and non-white people from the basic privileges of safety, liberty, and opportunity to thrive!"

The crowd cheers.

"It's not OK that white explorers arrived in this beautiful country and ignored those who were here first! They took our land away and tried to destroy our culture, our traditions, our way of life. It's not OK that they took our children! We must honour our treaties and continue to reconcile with our First Nations. Equality and respect are non- negotiable and we are tired of paying lip-service to the ideals of our charter!"

More cheers echo from the hundreds of faces standing before him.

"Poverty and homelessness matter! It's not OK to turn a blind eye to those who suffer. It's not OK to step over a homeless person in the street. Every person should have shelter! It's a basic human right and it needs to be treated that way! We demand social investments in housing, healthcare, and poverty!"

The crowd cheers loudly. "Homes for all! Homes for all! Homes for all!"

"That's right! You know this! Everyone deserves a home! What else do we know?

"We have learned the hard way that how we care for our planet matters! This generous planet cannot continue to sustain us any longer if we don't do our part. We don't need to consume and consume and consume. Not only is it unnecessary—it's harmful! We are in an environmental emergency! We cannot continue to take from our generous provider. Environmental collapse is inevitable and anyone who cannot see that is blinded by greed. Those people don't deserve to lead. They should not receive the privilege of governing our fine people and beautiful planet. They are not qualified! We have to stop them now! The earth is being destroyed by fire, floods, and superstorms. We have altered the climate! We need to stop killing our planet!"

"People and planet! People and planet! People and planet! People and planet! People and planet! People and planet!" the crowd chants.

The chanting continues for several minutes. Jonathan walks along the stage and chants with them.

"So, I have mentioned a lot of don'ts here today," he says. "Now I want to mention a couple of the dos. What we want to do is honour those who are doing it right. We honour those in positions of trust who have developed respect for everyone, who have learned patience, who have learned how to de-escalate and respect diversity, and who have lived a full, not a privileged, life. There is a difference! We honour those who do it right and put them in positions they deserve. You have to earn respect and positions of trust! You have to think of everyone's interests ahead of your own. Some people just don't get that. And those people should not be leaders."

The crowd cheers.

"We understand what's at stake. You know and I know what we have to do. It is our duty now to ensure the right people are working for us. Governance is supposed to work for the best interests of all of us—yours and mine, not just five or ten percent of us."

The crowd cheers again.

"I'm here to tell you, at this unique time of reckoning, that this is your country! Your lives do matter. Your priorities matter. The planet, healthcare, education, poverty reduction, and diversity matters!

"I am so very proud to live and work during this time of beautiful pushback. This time of reckoning! Please do not stop! Continue pushing for fairness, compassion, and justice until you get it. I will be right there at your side!"

Cheers, chanting, and applause transcends the street and expands in a wave of human spirit and hope that can be heard from blocks away. Lisa, Bethany, and Daiji are sitting to the side of the stage with a clear view of Jonathan. Daiji smiles with his eyes closed. Lisa and Jake hold hands, proud of their candidate and his heartfelt words.

Deep in the crowd, two weathered, tattered men stand silently, listening to the enthusiastic candidate. A brother's pain and struggle are temporarily lifted as he is transported to a place of pride, hope, and overwhelming joy.

"I believe in us. I believe in the power of our voices," says Jonathan. "You know, an elder once told me and my brother that even though life is unfair because of the colour of our skin, our culture, our name, and the mistakes we have made, we still have the power to choose. It's the only power we have—to let go of pain and choose to live in the exception.

"My mother was Cree. She met my father here on the west coast of British Columbia, and together they searched for

mino-pimatisiwin—the good life. Sadly, they didn't find it. Society was cruel to them. Treated them like their lives didn't matter. The same way our residential schools tried to treat us. I don't know about you, but I believe we deserve better than that. I believe our lives matter and we must choose differently. We deserve the good life. So, my friends, to all of you listening—let go of hate and struggle and choose the good life for all of us!"

Jonathan puts down his microphone, takes out his small carving, presses it to his lips, and stands with arms raised in solidarity with his audience.

Far out, at the furthest reaches of the stage, an old man in dirty clothes with tears streaming down his cheeks raises his arms and shouts back at his younger brother. "*Mino-pimatisiwin*, Robbie!"

My Pig Won

Sunday morning's sunny skies are a welcome relief. The Director and Henry are up early and have been walking and talking, energized by the sun. The Director has a new bounce in his step. His ballot was cast, and he is inspired by the popular candidate. Henry, too, was touched.

"You know him, RJ, don't you? Who is this Jonathan Richards? What nation is he from? He is a good talker. Do you believe him? He looks familiar."

"Yes, I believe him, Henry. He used to have a different name when I knew him. He had to change it when he was a boy."

"Who is he?"

The Director stops at a red-brick building. He bends outside the window of the café and picks up a butt.

"I got a good snoff here, Henry."

The café is bustling. A group of people are sitting inside, watching the local news. More people pile in. It looks like a party.

"Look, it must be someone's birthday in there," says Henry. "Oh, they're watching the TV. Look, it's on TV."

The Director and Henry peer into the café window at the TV screen. Jonathan Richards has been elected! The new candidate beats the incumbent. The people inside are raising their glasses and cheering.

"Your pig won!" shouts Henry.

"My pig won!" shouts the Director.

Henry and the Director embrace and dance around in a circle, oblivious to the attention they have attracted from inside the café. A young Indigenous woman nudges the man beside her and points to the window. For a moment, everyone in the café shares the joy of the two long-haired, dishevelled men outside.

"They are happy for you, Jonathan," says Molly, the owner of the Cloudberry Café.

Daiji gets up from his seat and walks toward the window. He stops directly in front of the glass and smiles at the two men. Molly steps up next to him at the window. "Let's invite them in, give them some coffee and breakfast," she says.

The Director and Henry stop their dancing and notice the attention they have attracted. Jonathan and Bethany stand next to Daiji and wave at the two men.

The Director sees Jonathan at the window. The two men look deep into each other's eyes with a shock of recognition. In disbelief, Jonathan gasps, filled with emotion. "It can't be," he whispers.

"What is it?" asks Bethany.

The Director and Jonathan gaze at each other through the glass. Years of memories flood Jonathan's head. Tears fall from his older brother's eyes, dripping onto the cigarette butt between his lips.

"Jonathan, what's wrong?" Bethany says again.

Jonathan runs outside.

"Jimmy, is it you?" he cries. "It's you! It's you! I have been looking for you for so long! Are you OK?"

"Robbie, my boy! Yes, I'm OK. I'm more than OK! Look at you! You did it! All by yourself, you did it! I'm sorry, Robbie. I'm sorry for all of it."

"You have nothing to be sorry for, Jimmy. You saved me so many times! None of this would have happened without you!"

Jimmy steps back and lays his hands on his brother's shoulders.

"I came back, Robbie. You must believe me. I came back to tell the truth. But then I saw them, all of them around you. The police, the elders. People were patting you on the back and smiling. You were OK. More than OK. You had people in your life who cared about you, so I left."

"I know you did. You were at the park. I saw you!"

"Yes, you did. I knew you did, but I didn't want to cause any more trouble for you and Lisa."

Lisa races outside, recognizing her brother in the old man.

"Jimmy!" she shouts and hugs her brother.

Henry stands there in disbelief, wiping his eyes.

"We are free, Jimmy. We are free!" says Jonathan.

"Everything is going to be OK."

"*Mino-pimatisiwin*!" says Jimmy, hugging his brother close.

In the last fifty years, Canada's homeless population has exploded. They stretch for blocks on Vancouver's East Hastings Street, take refuge under bridges in Toronto's downtown, and succumb to the cold in the Canadian prairies. A dependence on substances may be the beginning—or a consequence. Selling sex is all that's left.

Some live in a world of paranoia and delusion, while others escape abuse. Asylum-seekers desperately knock on any door that will answer, and the world's Indigenous peoples are denied again. First come is not always first served. Time and time again, we are told that if you aren't white, you don't matter. If you have experienced trauma, you don't matter. If you are poor, you don't matter. The cold, hard truth is that our most vulnerable are treated poorly.

Our planet serves as a mirror. Fires and floods ravage our land, leaving humans and animals searching for safer ground. The oceans are rising, and the atmospheric layers are thinning out.

So far, our response has been one of convenience and greed. Knee-jerk at best. Unexceptional.

We can respond differently.

Acknowledgements

I would like to acknowledge the Nuu-chah-nulth, Coast Salish, and Kwakiutl peoples of the Pacific coast, both past and present, who are keepers of the land where this story is based. I would also like to pay respect to the Cree nation and all peoples who strive for *mino-pimatisiwin* despite the barriers placed before them. I extend that respect to Michael A. Hart, the author of *Seeking Mino-pimatisiwin: An Aboriginal Approach to Helping,* for sharing with students like me the importance of this approach in all aspects of living.

CPSIA information can be obtained
at www.ICGtesting.com
Printed in the USA
LVHW100932250122
709124LV00032B/523